# The Billionaire's Cure

## Clean Billionaire Romance

# Penelope Spark

D1521516

1

Chad's teeth hurt. This happened whenever he got super annoyed. Why had he agreed to this ridiculous week? *You had no choice*, he reminded himself. But isn't there always a choice? Isn't that how he'd built his empire? By making choices? Was it arrogant to call it an empire? Probably. His company then—his *giant* company.

He looked out the car's window and watched the Maine forest speed by. It seemed they had been on this dirt road forever. The Uber driver had expressed concern when Chad had given him the address, but Chad had promised him a giant tip. That was two hours ago. Now they were on a dirt road that seemed to go on forever and got narrower and bumpier as they went. He'd been watching the GPS on his phone until he'd lost the signal. But he knew this would happen. The Serenity Hills website had promised this lack of cell service as if it were a selling point.

To his mentor, Saul, who had sent him to this remote godforsaken "haven," no cell service probably *was* a selling point.

*Serenity Hills*. Sounded like a nursing home. Or a cemetery. Or a nursing home with attached cemetery. Whatever this place was, he was *not* looking forward to learning more.

He just wanted to go home and get back to work.

"Are we lost?" he asked the driver in a terse tone.

"I don't see how. There's only one road." Mr. Uber didn't seem to be having much fun either.

Chad was considering telling him to turn around, abandon the whole quest, when they finally saw a sign.

"There it is," Mr. Uber said.

The wooden sign was small, and the colors were faded. Chad was certain it had been painted by children. "Welcome to Serenity Hills—where peace reigns." Chad didn't like the slogan. It reminded him that he *wasn't* holding the reins at the office right now.

"You need to *unplug*," Saul had said. The word "unplug" made him feel sick to his stomach. He *liked* being plugged in. Unplugged gadgets got no juice, collected dust, and got lost and forgotten.

Mr. Uber carefully pulled his car onto the narrow drive, which was a twisting steep climb. They passed small, almost dilapidated buildings along the way. Tiny, hand-painted wooden signs labeled each building: massage, meditation, sauna, art studio, and yoga. The yoga sign was crooked. He'd never actually tried yoga, but he was pretty sure he hated it.

Maybe the sign did too.

Finally, the road ended in a small, empty parking lot.

"Lots of people here," Mr. Uber said.

*Mr. Uber is trying to be funny.* Wordlessly, Chad handed him a wad of cash and climbed out of the car. Uber man stayed where he was, comfy in the driver's seat, and Chad was annoyed that he would have to get the luggage out of the trunk himself. Why hadn't he taken a cab? Normally he would've rented a car—he liked to stay in control of things—but Serenity Hills' website warned of limited parking, and specifically asked people not to bring cars if they could help it.

Now he thought they were just trying to make escape more difficult. He certainly wasn't going to take off on foot. They were at least fifty miles from a tar road. His mentor had called this place a resort. This was so *not* a resort. Why couldn't he have gone to a regular, *real* resort to relax and recharge?

Chad heard someone coming and looked to his left. A woman wearing a lot of brightly colored fabric and an inappropriately large smile said, "Hello, Chad! May I call you Chad?"

He nodded.

"My name is Naihma. May I give you a hug?"

The question surprised him, and as he hesitated, she came closer.

He took a step back. "Maybe later."

"I understand. Would you like to invite your friend in for refreshment?" She nodded toward the still closed driver side door.

"He's not my friend. He's the Uber driver."

"Oh. What's his name?"

Chad scowled. "I don't know."

"You don't know his name? Didn't you just spend two hours with him? It's a long trip up from Portland." She was still smiling, but her disapproval rolled off her in waves. She walked over to his window and rapped on it softly.

He rolled it down.

Naihma bent to peer through the window. "Hello there! What is your name?"

Chad couldn't hear his response.

"Hi, Oliver. So nice to meet you. Would you like to come inside for some refreshments?"

She paused, and then, "I understand." She looked at Chad. "He's waiting for you to shut the trunk."

*Oh!* Chad quickly slammed the trunk shut, and then Oliver hit the gas so hard, his tires spun up dirt behind them. *Good thing that didn't hit me, Mr. Oliver Uber.*

"Won't you come inside?" Naihma said, still wearing that ridiculous smile.

He grabbed his suitcase and trudged up the steep path behind her. "Not many people here?"

"Not right now," she said without turning around. "You are currently our only guest." She opened the door and motioned for him to step inside first, which he did. He was hit by the overwhelming smell of cloves.

"Someone got a toothache?" he asked.

"What?" She looked at him, obviously not getting his joke. Then, "Oh, I understand. No, we diffuse clove oil in this room. It is purifying and sends stress right out the window." Her voice increased in speed and pitch as she made this declaration, and as she spoke the last few words, she swung her arm dramatically toward the nearest window. Then she tittered.

"Oh." He couldn't think of anything else to say. He still wanted to go home.

"Come right this way. I want to introduce you to the family!"

*The family?* He followed her into another room, a larger space with lots of well-worn, but plush and inviting furniture. This room smelled like cinnamon. Despite himself, it smelled good. Inviting even. He scanned the faces in the room, and came to one that was disarmingly cute.

## 2

Heidi hadn't expected him to be so handsome. But as soon as she had the thought, she banished it from her head. No getting involved with clients, especially rich snotty ones. And even if she *did* allow her mind to go there, this guy was a billionaire. No *way* would he be interested in her. Still, when his eyes rested on her, a quiver ran through her stomach. She gave him a sincere smile that he didn't return. *See?* she told herself. *Rich and snotty.*

Naihma began her introductions, though no one moved from their seats.

"This is Meetika," Naihma said. "She is our gardener. So most of the food you'll eat here has been grown by her, completely organically, and with lots of love."

Chad nodded to Meetika. "You have an interesting name."

"It means soft-spoken," Naihma said. "And mine means peace."

Chad furrowed his brow. "Oh, so those aren't your *real* names?"

Meetika smiled broadly. "They are now."

Naihma, ignoring his question, continued with the introductions. "And this is Fawsa. She is our counselor—"

"What does Fawsa mean?" Chad asked with a bit of a sneer.

*Okay, he's growing less handsome by the minute.*

"It means triumph!" Fawsa exclaimed and shot one fist into the air.

Chad rolled his eyes.

"And this is Aakesh. He's in charge of buildings and maintenance. He's also our meditation coach."

"Of course he is. And what does Aakesh mean? Daydream?"

Aakesh smiled, though Heidi knew he was faking it. He wasn't much of a smiler, even when he wasn't being openly mocked by a new client. "It means sky. Openmindedness. Welcome to Serenity Hills."

Chad looked at Heidi. "And what's your name? A-kin-o-bam-pot-toy?"

Heidi dropped the smile. "I'm Heidi. Nice to meet you."

Chad's cheeks flushed red. This brought Heidi tremendous satisfaction.

"Sorry, folks." Chad looked at the floor. "I know this is what you do here, but well, this isn't my thing. I'm here against my will."

"We know that," Naihma said. "But sometimes where you don't want to be is right where you need to be. Now, are you hungry?"

Chad looked relieved. "I am."

"Great," Naihma said. "Heidi will show you to the kitchen."

*I will? Why me?* Heidi forced a smile and stood. "Right this way," she said and led him through the house to the kitchen.

"Hi, Bob," she said, when they got there. "This is our new guest, Chad."

"Hi, Chad! Nice to meet you!" Bob stuck out a hand, which Chad shook. Then Bob immediately went to the sink to wash his hands. "Would you like some sustenance?"

"Yes, please. That would be great. Thanks."

"My pleasure." Bob dried his hands, opened the fridge, and removed a giant bowl full of orange and green stuff. "We don't let anyone go hungry around here."

Heidi's mouth watered. This particular concoction was one of her faves.

Bob spooned a generous portion onto a plate and handed it to Chad, who took it tentatively.

"What is this?"

"Moroccan raw carrot salad."

Heidi was enjoying Chad's horror more than she should. "May I join you?"

He nodded absently.

She gave Bob a smile and a nod that said, "One for me too, please."

Bob obliged.

Heidi pulled out a high back stool for Chad. There was a large table in the room, but just the two of them fit nicely at the island where

Bob was working. "Have a seat." She patted the cushioned stool. He sat, looking reluctant. She sat beside him. When she did, her bare leg accidentally brushed against his pants, and sent a wave of butterflies through her stomach. She would have to put a stop to that. The guy wasn't *that* handsome.

As Chad pushed his food around in the bowl, Heidi dug into hers.

"As delicious as always, Bob!"

Chad looked at her in wonder and then took a bite himself. He chewed slowly, swallowed, and said, "It's very crunchy."

Heidi laughed. "Raw carrots usually are."

They ate in silence for a minute, and then Chad said, "Which meal is this?"

Bob looked at him, confused.

"I mean, it's still afternoon. So this is lunch, right? I was just hoping there will be a dinner. If this is the last meal of the day, I might starve."

Bob flinched.

"No, no!" Chad held up a hand. "I'm not insulting your salad. It's very good ... for carrots. I'm just hoping there will be some meat in my future."

Bob visibly recoiled at the suggestion.

Heidi, without thinking, put her hand on Chad's leg, but then yanked it away. Her cheeks grew hot, and she stammered to cover her faux pas. "We don't serve meat here. We only eat raw, living foods."

Chad looked as though he'd just found out his dog died. "I suppose that means the mashed potatoes and gravy are out?"

"Don't worry," Heidi said. "You won't believe how amazing you will feel. The electricity of these foods is through the roof, and your body is going to respond magnificently."

Chad didn't look convinced. "And what is your role here at Serenity Hills?"

"I'm the health coach."

He snickered. "And what online course qualifies you to be giving health advice?"

Heidi forced a smile. "I have a bachelor's degree in community health and a master's degree in nutrition."

## 3

Chad *had* to stop putting his foot in his mouth. *I'm going to have to live with these nuts for a week. I need to stop offending them. It's not their fault I'm here.*

"I'm sorry," he said again, and meant it. This woman seemed very nice, if not a little fruity. "I'm not usually such a jerk. I just really don't want to be here."

Bob plunked a glass in front of him. "Have some fresh pineapple juice. It will cheer you up."

Chad sincerely doubted that. He didn't want pineapple juice unless it was in a piña colada, but he took a drink anyway, and it was *delicious.* He drank some more, and then couldn't stop himself. He drained the glass, and then wiped his lips, a little embarrassed. "That's amazing."

Bob lit up. "Really hits the spot, doesn't it? Would you like some more?"

Chad nodded. It *had* cheered him up. How bizarre. "Thank you."

"Don't thank me. It's Heidi's recipe."

Chad picked up the now refilled glass. "Recipe? Isn't it just pineapple juice?"

"Pineapple juice, turmeric root juice, and dandelion greens juice. All raw. All as fresh as possible. The dandelions were harvested locally." He pointed out through a window, toward an overgrown lawn.

Doubt flickered through Chad's mind, but he dismissed it. The stuff was delicious. Who cared if there were weeds in it?

"Turmeric cures everything," Heidi said. "Anxiety, heart disease, arthritis ... even jerkhood."

Chad looked at her quickly. He hadn't expected such sass. She was different from the rest somehow. A little snarkier. He looked at Bob. "So how come you two don't have weird hippie names?"

Bob laughed and shrugged. "I'm happy with just Bob."

Chad looked at Heidi. "And you?"

Heidi wiggled her nose, a gesture that made her look a little like a rabbit, and magnified her cuteness. "I thought Heidi *was* a hippie name."

He didn't know how to respond to that, so he tackled the rest of his vegan carrot concoction in silence, and though his taste buds weren't satisfied, his stomach filled before he finished his serving. He pushed the bowl away and wiped his lips with a napkin Bob had recently provided. "My compliments to the chef. I cared for that far more than I expected to."

Heidi gave him a sideways smile. "I expect you'll be saying that a lot in the next week."

Chad blinked. Was she flirting? Might as

well flirt back, right? "You expect I'll be saying which thing? Compliments to the chef or caring more than I expect?"

She actually winked. "Both."

Wowsa. This girl was full of verve. Never mind that. He didn't have time for women, for love, for any distractions. Steering clear of such things was how he had stayed focused all these years, how he had become so successful. *Women weaken legs*. He grinned, remembering one of his favorite lines from *Rocky.* And even if he *did* make room for a relationship in his life, certainly this woman was not the one. She was a *health nut* for crying out loud. And she lived in the middle of godforsaken nowhere—

"What are you smiling about?" She interrupted his reverie.

His cheeks grew warm, but he'd been smiling about his favorite Rocky moment, not her. He hadn't been smiling about her—had he? "I was thinking about a movie I like." *Wow. Could I be any lamer?*

"Oh yeah? What movie's that?"

He was suddenly very embarrassed to be a *Rocky* fan. Did being a *Rocky* fan make him sound old? He hadn't even been born when it came out. "*Rocky*," he finally managed, after an elongated pause.

Her face lit up. "Ah, *Rocky*! I love those

movies. I grew up on them, because my dad loved them."

His dad had loved them too.

"Which one was your favorite?" she asked.

"Definitely the first. Though, I really enjoyed *Creed*."

Her face lit up. "I *loved Creed*! I was actually cheering out loud in the theater, as if I was really at a fight!" She laughed. "What a great character. Rocky was all heart. Are you all heart, Chad?"

He had no idea what to say to that. "Uh … sometimes."

She laughed. "Would you like me to show you to your room?"

"Absolutely." The idea brought him tremendous relief. He wanted to hide in his room. Shut the door and pull the curtains. Then pull the covers over his head. As soon as                                        possible.

## 4

Heidi led Chad to his room, far too aware of him walking right behind her. She could practically feel the energy coming off his body. *What is it about this guy? I need to get a grip.*

She stopped in front of the bathroom. "This is a communal restroom, but since you're the only one here right now, it's all yours."

He peeked inside, but didn't say anything.

She took another few steps down the hallway and swept her arm toward an open doorway. "Welcome. Make yourself at home."

"Thank you," Chad said, and rolled his suitcase into the room. As he walked by her, she caught a scent of him. He smelled like Christmas—like mint and fir needles. "So how long do I have?"

She didn't know what he meant. "I'm sorry?"

"How long before something happens?"

She thought she understood then. "Oh, you mean like a schedule?"

He nodded, and the intensity of his gaze unnerved her. He was making eye contact, but it was more than that. It felt as though he was looking right *into* her. And his eyes were so dark. Like good chocolate. She averted his gaze and looked out his window.

"Yes, a schedule," he said. "I'm wondering when I need to be somewhere next."

She forced herself to look at him again. She didn't want to be rude. "You have absolutely no schedule. You can do whatever you want and go wherever you want. If you want to meet with the counselor, find Fawsa. If you want to do some yoga, find me. If you want a massage, find Naihma. If you want some juice or food, go to the kitchen."

He raised an eyebrow. "The kitchen is always open?"

"Absolutely. We don't believe in prescribed mealtimes. You can eat when you're hungry, or when you want to eat. If Bob's there, he'll make you something, but if he's not there, there is always food in the fridge."

His face actually relaxed. "I kind of like that idea. But I'm surprised you let people eat whatever they want. Isn't this a health retreat?"

"It's nearly impossible to overeat when the only foods available to you are raw fruits and vegetables."

"Well, they may be raw, but can't I just sneak into the kitchen and cook some? Drown them in butter?" He laughed.

"We have no stove. And no butter. But other than whipping up some butter boiled cabbage, you are free to do what you want to do. Try to listen to your body and to your spirit and find out what you really need."

He rolled his eyes. "What I *need* is to answer some emails and make some calls."

She fought the urge to roll her eyes right back at him. "Actually, no you don't." She stepped back and turned to go. "If you need anything, find Naihma or anyone else. And really, we are here to help you, so don't be shy."

He looked around the room, and then chuckled, but it sounded humorless. "I have no idea what to do with myself."

It occurred to her then that this man might not know how to do nothing. Maybe he hadn't done nothing for a long time. "Chad?"

He looked at her.

"When's the last time you just sat still and did nothing?"

He shrugged. "On the airplane, when I was asleep?"

She shook her head slowly. "That doesn't count, because you were sleeping. Sleeping is doing something. I mean when was the last time you sat and did *nothing*? Absolutely nothing. Looked at the sky? Watched a bird? Closed your eyes and felt the sun on your face? Smelled some wildflowers?"

He looked contemplative and let out a long breath. "I don't know. Maybe not since I was a kid. Time is money, so I try not to waste it."

She stepped toward him again. "I don't want

to argue with your philosophy, Chad. It has obviously served you well financially, but time is *not* money. You can always make more money. You only get so much time."

He blinked as if he'd never heard such a thing, but he didn't argue.

She took this as a win.

"Okay then," he said. "I think I will go outside and do nothing. Maybe sniff some wildflowers."

Her smile erupted. "Awesome. Enjoy them. The lupines are my favorite."

He snickered. "Lupines. Sounds like a name for one of your staff members."

She didn't laugh. She'd heard similar jokes before from guests far funnier.

He looked a smidge ashamed of his attempt at humor. "Which ones are the lupines?"

"The tall purple ones." She turned to go.

"Hey, Heidi?"

She turned back. She liked the way her name sounded in his voice. "Yeah?"

"Thank you. I mean it. I can see already that you're a good health coach. I'm sorry if I doubted you earlier."

*Maybe he isn't such a jerk after all.* "No problem. I know you're under a lot of stress, and I know you don't really want to be here. But try to enjoy yourself. It will be really, *really* good for you. I've seen lots of people like you come through here"—she stopped and corrected herself—"well, they're not usually as *rich* as you, but successful business people like yourself, and they really benefit from slowing down."

He looked out the window. "I don't know. Slowing down makes me feel like I'm wasting time, like I'm going to miss something."

She gave him a smile she hoped was reassuring. "I think the opposite is true. We don't miss things when we go slowly. We miss things when we're going too fast."

## 5

Chad awoke and sat up with a start, sure he had overslept. Then he realized where he was—hippie camp—and lay back down. He had no idea what time it was, but the sun was shining strong through his window, so it wasn't early. *It's hot in here*. He threw the covers off and looked around for a clock. Of course, there wasn't one. He was on hippie time here. He found the slacks he'd worn yesterday and rescued his cell from a pocket. It was quarter after nine. He hadn't slept that late in years. Maybe ever. And with this thought, he realized how *well* he'd slept. It had taken him forever to actually fall asleep, but once he did, *wow*. It had been so quiet.

He wanted to take a shower, but first things first. Coffee. He couldn't believe he didn't have a headache yet—he was usually on his fourth latte by now—but he knew a headache was coming. So he put on his vacation clothes, jeans, T-shirt, and flip-flops, and, marveling at how comfortable they were, tried to navigate his way back to the kitchen.

"Good morning, Chad!" Bob cried when Chad arrived at his destination.

*He can't possibly be that excited to see me.*

When Chad entered the kitchen, Heidi had her back to him, but she turned around when she heard his name. His heart leapt at the sight of her. He couldn't believe his own response to her and tried to push it down. Didn't even want to go there.

"Good morning, Chad!" she echoed. She sounded equally as excited. He wondered then how many guests they had. Maybe he was the first they'd had in months. Maybe they were really bored.

"Morning," he managed, not even coming close to matching their enthusiasm. "Is there coffee?"

Heidi looked regretful.

*Oh no. Is there no coffee? There isn't, is there? Health nuts don't drink coffee. I'm going to die. The health nuts are going to kill me.*

"We don't serve coffee, but I can brew you some yerba maté if you like," Bob said.

"Yerba maté?" Chad repeated, incredulous. "Is that like a latte?" He didn't think there was much chance of this being true, but hey, maté and latte rhymed.

Bob chuckled. "Not quite. But you'll love yerba maté. It's incredibly delicious, healthy, and has a good dose of caffeine."

Chad slid onto a stool at the island in the center of the brightly lit room. "Well, then of course, I'll try some yerba maté. But if you serve caffeine, why don't you just serve coffee?"

Heidi flitted over and sat on the stool beside him. She winked. "It's not the caffeine in coffee that kills you."

"Oh yeah? Then what is it?"

"Everything else."

He thought she was chock-full of baloney, but he held his tongue.

"So," she said, leaning toward him. "How did you sleep?"

Longingly, he watched Bob slowly dump what looked like some dried out leaves and twigs into a cloth tea bag. What were they trying to do to him? He looked at Heidi. "It took me a long time to fall asleep, but once I was able to pull the trigger, I slept great."

"Awesome. I'm sure your body is thrilled. You'll probably fall asleep more easily tonight, but just in case, I'll make you some herbal tea."

He raised an eyebrow. "More dandelions?"

She giggled. "I can certainly include dandelions if you like."

Bob turned toward them. "Heidi is an accomplished herbalist. She can whip you up a concoction that'll knock you out cold."

"Don't let him alarm you," Heidi rushed to say. "I've studied herbs a lot. You are in safe hands."

Somehow, Chad knew this was true. "Got any herbs for high blood pressure?"

"Of course I do." She jumped up. "Let me get you some ginger juice, and then—"

"Ginger *juice*?"

Bob grinned. "It's a little like drinking fire. You're going to love it."

*Sure.*

"I'll mix it with some apple juice," Heidi said. "And hang on. I'll go get you some Pipsissewa."

"Pip-sis-a-what?"

She either didn't hear him or ignored him.

He looked at Bob. "It's safe to do what she says?"

Bob nodded. "Absolutely. I don't think that woman has ever been sick in her life." Bob set a steaming cup of brown liquid in front of Chad.

"Thanks," Chad said, unsure if he was truly thankful.

"Would you like any coconut milk? Or honey?"

Chad shuddered. "I don't think so. No thanks." He blew into the cup and then took a tentative sip. Huh. That wasn't so bad. It was no latte, but it had potential. He took another sip.

By his fifth sip, he could feel the caffeine working its way toward his brain. "Can I get some more of this?"

"Coming right up!" Bob spun around to heat

some more water.

Heidi reappeared then with a small bag full of more twigs and dried leaves. "Pipsissewa," she said. "The name is Cree for 'break into little pieces.'" So she had heard him. "Because it breaks kidney stones into little passable pieces."

Chad looked up at her. "But I don't have kidney stones."

She gave him a knowing look that he found both patronizing and somehow alluring. "So you think."

"But if I do, can't we leave them where they are? They're not bothering anyone."

She didn't say anything, so he added, "I'm not sure I want to pass them." He was genuinely afraid of her herbology.

She smiled at him. "That's why we're going to break them into small pieces first."

Chad looked at Bob, wondering why he wasn't stepping in to rescue him.

"It's also good for blood pressure," Heidi added.

"And what am I supposed to do with pip-sis-a-na?"

"*Pipsissewa*," she said again, over-enunciating. "I'm going to make you a tea."

Chad looked down at the beverage in front of him. He was going to be well hydrated.

"Do you want any food to go with your

beverages?" Bob asked.

"More carrots?"

Bob chuckled. "How about a berry pomegranate bowl?"

That actually didn't sound so bad. "Sure. Thanks." It wasn't that Chad was *opposed* to eating healthy. He just never really had time. Often, he neglected to eat at all.

Bob dug into the fridge while Heidi set another steaming mug in front of him. "Let that steep for five minutes and then enjoy. But be warned—pipsissewa can make your pee green."

"Fantastic." Serenity Hills was introducing him to all sorts of new life experiences.

"I put some Siberian ginseng in there too. It'll lower your blood pressure, and it also helps relieve stress." She winked. "You can't heal the body selectively."

*Whatever that means.*

She must have read his confusion. "What I mean is, when you try to heal part of your body, you automatically affect every other part of your body. So as you're working on lowering your blood pressure, the rest of you will be positively affected as well. Heal your kidneys, your blood pressure improves. Heal your liver, your skin clears up." A hand flew to her mouth. "Not that there's anything wrong with your skin," she said quickly. "It's lovely."

She flushed a deep red.

Chad was beyond amused. "Thanks, I guess." He wanted to rescue her. "My liver could probably use some work."

She looked grateful. "Oh yeah, why's that?"

"I drink a bit."

Her face fell.

"Not much," he hurried to add. "I don't get drunk or anything. I just have trouble relaxing, so I have a drink or two before I go to bed—"

"Every night?"

He shrugged. "Usually."

"Wow, no wonder you had trouble falling asleep last night."

*Yeah. That. Among other things.*

## 6

"Now what?"

*Why does he keep asking me that?* Heidi thought. *I'm not his taskmaster.* "I don't know. What do you want to do?"

"I *want* to call the office and check in. But I'm told that's not allowed?"

"No, sorry. You're here to rest. If we let you work, you wouldn't be able to rest."

He took another bite of his pomegranate seeds and then looked contemplative as he chewed. "Then I don't know. What do most people do their first morning here?"

"It varies. Some people jump right into the yoga and massage. Some people spend time alone, in their rooms, or outside sitting in the sun. We have lots of hammocks around the property. Some people talk to Fawsa."

He scrunched up his face, making it clear that wasn't his first choice.

"Some people read. We have lots of books in the library. And some go for walks. We have lots of trails—"

"A walk! Yes! Let's do it!"

Wait, what? She hadn't said *she* would go for a walk, just that it was an option for *him.* "Uh ..."

"Just give me a few minutes to finish eating these little red things, and to drink this ...

um"—he looked down at her herbal tea— "*potion*, and then I'll go get my tennis shoes on."

"I'm an herbalist, not a magician, and that's not a potion." She looked down, embarrassed of the snippiness in her voice. Why had she gotten so defensive?

He didn't respond, and the silence unnerved her, so she looked up at him. When she did, they made eye contact, as if he'd been waiting for her to look at him before speaking. "Sorry. Really. I didn't mean anything by it. I think I was trying to be funny. So, about that walk? Can you wait for me to get my feet dressed?"

She fumbled for words. "Okay, sure, well, no hurry. The trails aren't going anywhere. Take your time."

He took another bite, and as he chewed, he looked down at her feet. "Are you going to wear those?" She looked down at her flip-flops and was suddenly embarrassed. She'd already been out in the garden that day harvesting chamomile blossoms, and her feet showed the evidence. *He must be horrified. He's probably used to women who get expensive pedicures and have purple toenails.* The only time she'd ever had purple toenails was the time she'd gotten lost snowshoeing. She shook her head. Why was she thinking such thoughts? Why did she care what this guy thought about her feet?

"You okay?"

She looked up and thought she saw genuine concern in his eyes. Bob was staring at her too.

"Uh … yeah … I'll go get some hiking boots on. I'll be right back." She turned and fled, almost smacking into Naihma in the hallway.

"What's on fire?"

"Huh?" Heidi didn't understand and didn't have the energy to try to figure out what she meant.

"You're in such a hurry, I figured there was a fire." Naihma smiled.

"Oh, no … I'm … I'm not in a hurry. I just need my boots."

Naihma furrowed her brow. "Boots?"

Heidi nodded and tried to walk by her.

Naihma stopped her by gently grabbing her arm. "I understand what has you in such a tizzy. It's Mr. LaChance, isn't it?"

Heidi's cheeks grew hot. "What? No! Of course not."

Half of Naihma's mouth curled up in a smile. She lowered her voice. "It's all right to be attracted to someone, Heidi. It's perfectly natural. We were created for relationship, you know."

"I am *not* attracted to him. First of all, he's a *client*. I would never. Second of all, he's *rich*."

Naihma barked out a laugh. "You say that like it's a horrid thing."

"Well, isn't it?"

"Not at all! It depends on how he got rich. If he's honest and hardworking, then all the power to him."

"That's not what I meant," Heidi said, but she didn't know how to explain herself. "I just mean we come from different planets. But it doesn't matter, because I'm not attracted to him."

Naihma stared at her.

"Honest," Heidi said, and almost believed it herself.

Naihma finally let her go, and Heidi hurried to her room and put on her hiking boots. She couldn't imagine Mr. City Slicker would want to do any actual *hiking*, but just in case, she'd be prepared. She rubbed Lavender oil all over her bare legs and then headed for the door. Then she thought better of it and went to the mirror.

She looked like she always looked. Light blonde wind-tousled wavy hair. More freckles than a gang of Walton children. No makeup in sight. She'd never wanted to wear makeup and never felt she needed it. So why was she suddenly wondering if she needed lip gloss? This was ridiculous. She smiled at herself in the mirror and said aloud, "You're absolutely beautiful just the way you are. Stop thinking foolish thoughts about a foolish man."

"Who's foolish?" a deep voice asked from her open doorway.

## 7

Heidi looked mortified, and Chad regretted saying anything to her. He hadn't meant to sneak up on her, startle her, or embarrass her.

"Uh, I was just doing my daily affirmations. I said foolish *tan* as in I wish I was more tan, not foolish man."

He knew, beyond a shadow of a doubt, that she was lying. She'd said "man," and the fact that she bothered to lie about it suggested she was talking about *him*. Why had she called him foolish, and why was she thinking about him? "Oh, well, I wouldn't say that at all. Your skin is perfect." It was his turn to be embarrassed. Why had he said such a thing?

She grabbed a small bottle off her dresser and held it out to him. "You might want to put this on your legs. It'll keep the ticks off you. Well, most of them anyway."

"Ticks?" The thought alone made him feel small legs skittering all over his skin.

"Yeah, they're really bad this year."

He was wearing jeans. Did she mean that she wanted him to hike up his pant legs and rub oil on his legs? As in right now? Standing in the doorway of her bedroom? Could this get any weirder? He tentatively reached for the bottle. She refused to move any closer to him, and he had to stretch to get his fingertips on the bottle. He almost fell into the room. Yep, this could get weirder.

He looked down at his own legs. "You want me to put it on my jeans? Or my skin?"

She laughed, seeming to finally realize that this scenario was a little absurd. "On your skin, a little above your socks. But you can put it on your jeans too if you like."

He unscrewed the cover, and for reasons that escaped him, sniffed the oil. "Whew!" he cried. "That is some potent stuff!"

"Of course. It takes about three pounds of lavender blossoms to make the oil in that bottle."

*That's a lot of flowers.* "Do you make the oil yourself?"

Her eyes widened as if that was a ridiculous question. "No, no. I don't have the necessary equipment."

"Ah, I see. Sorry, I made an assumption because there was no label on the bottle."

"Oh, yeah. I buy in bulk. Cheaper that way." She stood there staring at him expectantly.

*All right. Might as well get this over with.* He knelt on one knee and hiked up his pant leg. Then he began to perfume his ankle. "I can't believe I'm doing this. I'm going to smell so girly."

He hadn't meant to be funny, but a high-pitched giggle erupted out of Heidi, making him look up quickly to see what she was laughing at. The sight of her face all scrunched up in a laugh made him laugh too. And his laugh made her laugh even harder. Soon they were both gasping for air, and he wasn't even sure what he'd said that was so funny. He forced himself to get a grip and catch his breath, and then he stood up.

She made a squeaking sound that he thought was supposed to be words.

"What?"

She began to laugh even harder, but tried again to communicate. "Don't forget your other leg!" She forced the words out and then fell into another fit of giggles.

He shook his head, but knelt down to make his other ankle smell as girly as the first.

Finally, his ankles were adequately fragrant, and she followed him out of her room, down the hallway, and out into the sunshine. He couldn't help but notice that when the sunlight hit her, her hair seemed to transform into sunlight itself. He forced himself to look away before she could catch him staring.

"All right," she said, still sounding out of breath from all the laughing. "Which trail would you prefer? One beside a bubbling brook? Through meadows of wildflowers? Or through the forest?"

He had no idea. He'd never chosen a trail

before. "Which one's your favorite?"

She seemed to give that some deep thought. "We might as well stick to our theme. Let's go with the wildflowers."

"Wildflowers it is then." He followed her across the large yard toward what looked like a solid bank of trees. He felt a bit of anxiety about it. He never felt intimidated by anything, but the forest looked daunting, unwelcoming. Who was this woman, really? Was she qualified to be his guide? Did he really want to follow her into the wilderness? As they got closer to the woods, he saw the head of a trail and relaxed a little. There was a beaten path. He wouldn't have to leave breadcrumbs behind him to find his way home.

## 8

Heidi tried to think of something to say. This was an unusual urge for her. For starters, she was a chatty cathy, never at a loss for words. Second, she was also very comfortable with silence. So why wasn't she comfortable walking through the peaceful woods on this gorgeous morning with this gorgeous man? She shook her head. She had to *stop* thinking of him as gorgeous. It was true: he *was* gorgeous. But still. He was a client. Off limits. And he was also a billionaire from the big city. She was a free spirit from the woods. And she *liked* being a free spirit from the woods. This was the life she'd chosen for herself, and she loved it. She didn't want to change her life, no matter how handsome he was.

"Penny for your thoughts?"

She smiled at him. "I was just thinking how gorgeous everything is."

He scowled. "Really? Maybe I'm missing something. All I see are insects." He slapped at something on his neck.

"Sorry, should have added some citronella oil to your defense system. The mosquitoes hate the smell of it."

"These are mosquitos? I thought they were birds. Maybe baby eagles. With rabies."

She laughed. "People joke that the Maine

state bird is the mosquito. Remind me next time to give you some citronella oil." *Wait, what? Now he thinks I want to go on another walk with him.* "I mean … I just think you'd like the smell of citronella better than lavender. It doesn't smell as girly."

Golly, that had been funny. And she'd felt so much better after a good belly laugh. A grown man down on one knee whining about smelling "girly." Who even uses that word? Other than fifth graders on the playground.

"Yeah, I bet it's one of those really manly essential oils." He chuckled at his own joke. "I'm sorry, I've always thought essential oils were quackery. Something for suburban housewives to spend money on."

In other circumstances, this might have offended her, but the tone of his voice was so benign that she knew he hadn't meant anything by it.

"Oh no, they're the real deal. But I see your point. It is weird how popular they've gotten. I think that's due to some companies using multi-level marketing. But essential oils have been used for thousands of years. They're certainly no fad."

"You know about marketing?"

She scoffed. "Hardly. I wish we lived in a world without money."

It was his turn to scoff. "I hear people say

that, but no one seems to have any idea how that could possibly work."

"Easy. We build our own homes out of trees. We grow our own food. We work together to maintain our communities."

"And what if your kid needs medicine?"

She looked at him. "My kid? Do you have kids?"

"I don't. I was trying to emotionally charge my question." He chuckled.

"Well, that's the wrong question to use to convince me. I would just give him herbs."

"Ah, so your fictional child is a boy?"

They both laughed.

"So then name a material that you *do* want or need."

She was not going to take his bait. "I have everything I need already."

He looked annoyed, and she wondered if she should tone it down a notch. Then decided, *nah.* This was the real her, and he had invited her for the walk. He could always turn around if he wanted.

He looked down at her boots. "Okay, your boots. Those are nice boots. What did they cost you? Over a hundred bucks, right?"

"I got them at the thrift store, so no. They were about twenty."

He rolled his eyes. "Fine. Used boots. So you want to acquire someone's used boots, and you go to trade with them, but they don't want your herbs, or your juice, or your essential oils. They want fuel for their tractor. They won't give you the boots. In fact, they have no one to give the boots to because they can't find anyone with tractor fuel, because no one is willing to live on an oil rig when they're only going to get someone's cranberry jam for payment."

She laughed. "Cranberry jam? What is wrong with you?"

He smiled, and the sight of it made her stomach flip. His teeth were *perfect*. She nervously slid her tongue over her slightly crooked eye teeth.

"My point remains," he said.

She hadn't entirely followed his example, but she tried to pretend she had. "I would offer to clean their kitchen in exchange for their boots. Everyone wants a clean kitchen."

He threw his hands up. "Fine. I give up."

She was looking at him as she was walking and didn't see the giant root poking up through the path. Her toe banged into it, and her face was rapidly heading for the ground when strong hands grabbed her around her waist and pulled her up.

She couldn't believe how good those hands felt: firm, reliable, safe. She shook her head. "Thank you. I almost smashed my nose into the earth."

"You're welcome. I didn't want to have to watch you try to barter your dandelion greens in the emergency room."

She giggled. "Okay, okay. You've made your point."

They were still standing there, looking into each other's eyes, his hands still on her hips. It was suddenly incredibly awkward. He dropped his hands, and she started walking again. He followed behind at first and then came alongside her.

"So, how did you make your billion?"

He raised an eyebrow. "Who told you I made a billion?"

She thought for a second. "I don't remember. But we all knew before you got here. So someone must have known and then told the rest of us." She looked at him. "Sorry, I really don't remember."

"That's okay. It's not a secret. So I founded a company that provides products and services to help with sustainable agriculture."

She stopped walking and looked at him.

He stopped too. "What?"

"So you're a farmer?"

He laughed. "No, not really. I never get my hands dirty, and I don't drive a tractor, but I *did* grow up on my grandfather's farm in western Massachusetts. I watched him struggle with how fast the industry was changing. He was old school, wanted to do right by the earth, keep the soil healthy, keep the product healthy. And because he didn't buy into new methods, his business suffered. So I decided I wanted to make sustainable farming a profitable enterprise again." He gave her a sheepish smile. Was that a bit of humility she saw? "But I didn't want to actually farm. I thought it was too much work. Now I work as hard as any farmer, and probably harder than most."

"And that's how you ended up here." Heidi had already read his paperwork. She knew all about his condition.

"Yep. High blood pressure. Cortisol levels through the roof. Migraines that keep me from work. A while back, I hired an executive coach. His name is Saul, and he's like a mentor. My performance has improved drastically since he started helping me, and my company has grown in leaps and bounds, but my health has gotten worse. So, he's forcing me to be here."

"Forcing you?" She didn't understand how an executive coach, whatever that was, could force Chad to do anything.

"Yeah. He says if I don't get my health under control, he'll stop mentoring me. And I really don't want that to happen. He's helped so much. I've made a killing with his advice. And so, though this particular bit of advice I didn't really want to take, I'm taking it anyway. Saul says I'll be far more successful if I'm physically healthier."

"He's right."

He took a deep breath. "Maybe. But my health issues come from my stress issues. And I don't think herbs and sunshine are going to take away the stress of running a billion-dollar business." He swatted at another mosquito.

"Well, whoever sent you here, I'm glad you're here." *Oh no.* Had she really just said that? She'd meant to say, "*We're* glad you're here." Could she get any more embarrassed?

She noticed a mosquito on his upper arm, just under his sleeve, and without thinking, smacked it. A loud slap echoed through the woods. Chad recoiled, his eyes wide.

Yes, she could get more embarrassed. She sheepishly held up her hand, which had blood on it. "I got him," she said.

He grinned. "I guess you did. You really saved me."

She giggled sheepishly. "Let's keep walking. The bugs are less aggressive when we're moving."

"Really?"

"That's my theory, anyway."

He laughed. "Anyway, I don't want you to think I'm complaining. I chose this life for myself and I love it. The game of it. The competition. I thrive on the pressure."

"Right. But your body isn't designed to function at that speed all the time. You have adrenaline to help you through intense circumstances, not to propel you through every moment of every day. That's wearing your body down."

He nodded and said quietly, "I know."

She stopped again. "Here are the wildflowers."

He let out a low whistle. "Yeah, I guess that is pretty spectacular."

They stood there gazing for a moment, and Heidi noticed how happy she felt. And it wasn't just because of the wildflowers.

"And these just ... happened? You haven't done anything here?"

"Nope. I haven't done a thing. Sometimes things work out best if you just let nature take its course."

## 9

Chad needed a break from Heidi, so he headed for the sauna. He was enjoying her company too much. He was having thoughts and feelings that he shouldn't be having. *This is why I don't slow down*, he thought. Stop running, and the distractions come at you from all angles.

But gosh, she was so pretty. And *real*. As refreshing as clean ocean air. As refreshing as that pineapple juice Bob had fed him again at lunchtime. She made him feel more alive. She was real, and she made *him* feel more real.

All of this was wonderful, but he had to go back to his world in five days, his world that he built and that he loved. Maybe he could come back here every once in a while to recharge? As soon as he had the thought, he laughed at it. He hadn't wanted to come to Serenity Hills, had fought tooth and nail against it, and now here he was already thinking about coming back. This health coach had far too much power over him.

Hence, a trip to the sauna.

She'd told him it would be good to "sweat out" the toxins trapped in his lymphatic system. He didn't really know what that meant. He was more motivated to "sweat out" his crazy ideas about her. He hoped spending some time in a Finnish fire cabin would do the trick. He'd never been in a traditional sauna. This rickety shack looked nothing like the modern, sterile sauna he had at home.

Heidi had sent Aakesh ahead to get the sauna ready, and as Chad approached, he could see steam pouring out of the strange little shanty. Behind the sauna ran a bubbling brook. Heidi had given him explicit instructions: spend ten minutes in the sauna and then immediately run and jump into the brook. They had widened a small area of the brook to create a pool. At least, he assumed they had made the modification. Either that or mother nature had known they were going to build a sauna in that spot. The water would still only come up to his knees, so Heidi had told him to sit down in it. He had no intention of following her instructions. At all. Ever.

Aakash came around a corner, startling Chad. He was carrying a bouquet of tree branches.

"Howdy!" he cried.

Chad didn't respond.

"These are birch leaves," Aakash said, answering a question no one had asked, "and you'll want to hit your skin with them." He demonstrated, raising the branches up over his head and then banging himself on the back with them. It looked absurd.

"Why?" Chad asked.

"Tradition!" He banged the leaves on each of his arms.

Chad started to worry that Aakash was going to go into the sauna with him. So much for relaxing.

"It opens up the pores on your skin and releases the essential oils from the leaves."

*These people and their dang essential oils.*

He banged himself on each bare leg. "Would you like to do it? Or would you like me to help?"

By no means did Chad want this lunatic beating him with a birch tree. "No, no, I can do it!" He gingerly took the handful of branches from Aakesh, and then weakly slapped his knee with them.

"Harder!" Aakesh cried, but there wasn't an iota of sadism in his tone or his body language. He looked like a jolly Santa handing out Christmas gifts to children—except he was really skinny and really tan.

Chad whacked himself with more oomph.

"There you go! Good work! Make sure you get your back!"

Beyond annoyed with Aakesh's enthusiasm, Chad continued to slap himself until Aakesh determined he'd had enough and took the leaves away from him. Aakesh opened the sauna door, allowing more steam to pour out, and said, "Welcome! Step right in!"

The heat took Chad's breath away, but after a few seconds, it felt kind of good. He had a sauna at home, but he was pretty sure this one was hotter. He sat on a wooden bench and was immediately bored. To his dismay, Aakesh sat down on the bench across from him. At least he was giving him some personal space.

"I poured a bunch of water on the rocks," Aakesh said, "to boost the humidity. If it starts to feel too dry in here, let me know, and I will pour some more."

"It's fine," Chad said and leaned back. He closed his eyes, and immediately an image of Heidi popped into his head. He opened his eyes again. Why was he so fascinated by this woman? Immediately, he knew why. Because he was bored. Because here at Serenity Hills, there was nothing else to occupy his used-to-being-busy brain. He had nothing else to do. It occurred to him that when he left Serenity Hills and got back to his real life, he would forget all about the health coach.

This idea made him a little sad.

*Later,* he told himself. When he had met his business goals, *then* he could think about having a relationship. *We must be getting close to the ten-minute mark.* "How long have we been in here?"

Aakesh didn't open his eyes. "One and a half minutes."

Chad sighed. Patience had never been one of his strengths. In fact, his lack of it had served him well. It wasn't serving him well now. He tipped his head back and stared at the ceiling. Why had he agreed to this?

"If you get too hot, you *can* step out. Some people can't tolerate it."

Chad took this as a challenge to his toughness, to his manhood. "I can tolerate the heat," he said, his voice sounding defensive. "I'm just bored."

"Would you like me to lead you in guided meditation?"

"No thanks," Chad said quickly. He lay down on the bench and put his arm behind his head. This was surprisingly comfortable.

He was finally starting to relax when Aakesh said, "Time for the brook!"

Chad sat up. "I don't think I need the brook."

"Sure you do! It will close those pores right up and get your blood flowing. But again, you don't have to do anything you can't tolerate."

*Grr.* Why did this guy have to keep challenging his masculinity? Fine. He would do it. He followed Aakesh out the door and was dismayed to learn that his fearless leader was going to *run* to the brook. Chad would not run. He refused to look any more ridiculous than he already did, but followed at a brisk walking pace. He couldn't believe how cool the air felt. It was 85 degrees out. Aakesh sprinted and then splashed into the small pool; Chad followed with caution. The water was about fifty degrees colder than he'd expected, and it took every ounce of willpower he'd ever had to not turn and flee. Aakesh was already sitting on a rock, the cold water running past his neck. Chad took a deep breath and followed suit.

"How do you feel?" a familiar voice asked.

He looked up to see Heidi standing on the bank, smiling down at him.

*Good thing I didn't run away*, he thought.

## 10

Heidi bit back a laugh. She didn't want to embarrass Chad, but he looked so miserable—like a child being forced to eat Brussels sprouts. He did not answer when she asked him how he felt; he just gave her an exasperated look.

"Aakesh!" she called to her coworker, who was tipping his head back into the water and probably couldn't hear her.

He looked up, his face saying, "Did I just hear something?"

"Naihma called a family meeting."

"Right now?" He sounded so disappointed. Heidi knew Aakesh really enjoyed his icy plunges, especially when he could use them to impress guests.

"Right now. We have incoming."

Aakesh stood to climb out of the brook, and Chad sprang up to follow him. Aakesh looked at him. "You should do another round."

Chad nodded, but Heidi had a feeling another round wasn't in the cards.

Aakesh followed her, sans towel, all the way up to the main house. *Anywhere else, showing up to a staff meeting with your shorts dripping would probably be frowned upon.* She loved her job and loved the people she worked with. They were doing important stuff here: helping people get back to basics. Helping people to help themselves.

Meetika, Fawsa, and Naihma were already in the lounge. Bob was handing out juice.

"Does that juice have ginger in it, or are we diffusing ginger oil?" Heidi loved ginger.

"Both," Naihma declared and took an eager sip of the juice.

Bob handed Heidi a glass too, and she gulped some down before settling into a cushy armchair.

"We've got incoming," Naihma said.

"On a Monday?" Fawsa said.

Usually, guests arrived on a weekend. Many of them only stayed for a weekend. Heidi always felt bad for those visitors. Two days wasn't nearly long enough to recharge. As soon as they started to relax, it was time to jump up and go.

"Yes," Naihma said. "It seems it was a bit of a sudden decision. Gloria is a professional dancer, and she injured her hamstring in a performance yesterday, so, as she's forced to rest and heal that injury, she thought she'd rest and heal the rest of her."

Heidi's first thought was, *I hope she's not beautiful.* The thought made her quite angry with herself, and she shook her head, trying to expel it from her mind. Why would she think such a thing? Then she thought, *I hope she's old.*

*Heidi!* she silently chastised herself. *Get it together!*

Naihma was still talking. Gloria Davison was coming from Boston and would be arriving shortly. *Many* of their clients were from Boston, but this time, the fact made Heidi's stomach turn. She took a deep breath. Just because they had two guests from the same city didn't mean the two guests were going to automatically fall in love. In fact, the chances of that were pretty slim. And even if they *did* fall in love, wouldn't that be great for Chad? That could be exactly what he needed. She should *want* that to happen. Why was she trying to wish that away from him? It's not like *she* wanted to get involved with an emotionally unavailable rich snob who worked twenty-four hours a day, right? Right. Plus, he was a client. She closed her eyes and silently chanted a mantra: *I want him to be happy. I hope he and Gloria hit it off. I want him to be hap—*

"You all right, Heidi?" Naihma interrupted.

"Uh, yes!" Heidi's cheeks grew hot. She'd blushed more since Chad had arrived than she'd blushed all year.

"Great." Naihma didn't look convinced. "I was asking if you could prepare a pretty aggressive healing regimen for her. She says she needs her leg back in shape as quickly as possible. She's only staying until Saturday."

Heidi nodded. "I'm on it."

"Thank you," Naihma said. "Her file is in the office." She smiled at everyone. "That's all I have for you. I'll be getting her room ready if anyone needs me."

The meeting broke up, and Heidi headed for the main office. It had one of the few phones in the entire complex, and the only computer. She flicked on the light and fired up the old PC. As she waited for the computer to boot up, she read Gloria's file. There wasn't much in there. No details about her injury. The computer chimed that it was ready, and Heidi opened a browser window.

She tapped "Gloria Davison" into the search bar. The first few results were for a high school softball pitcher in Florida. Maybe Gloria wasn't so famous after all. She mentally kicked herself for having such a thought. What was wrong with her?

Their Gloria showed up in the fifth search result. Heidi clicked on the article, and a picture loaded. Her heart sank. Gloria was *gorgeous*. She was tall and slender, her body the epitome of grace, and her skin like porcelain. Nary a freckle in sight.

"Who's that?" a voice behind her asked.

She stabbed her mouse at the little black X

that would hide her investigation and whirled around. "Chad? What are you doing here?"

## 11

Chad hadn't meant to startle her and felt bad about it. But why was she acting as though she'd been caught with her hand in the till? "Sorry, didn't mean to scare you."

"No problem. But you're not supposed to be back here."

He took a step back, holding his hands up in surrender. "Sorry again. I just wanted to find you, and Naihma said you were probably in here. You okay?"

"Yeah." She stood up. "Why did you need to find me? How can I help you?"

She still looked upset, and he felt an overpowering urge to fix whatever was wrong, but in that moment, he didn't have the energy. "I feel like I'm dying." Some combination of birch oil, Aakesh, intense heat, and freezing cold had put him on the fast track toward death.

"Does your head hurt?"

He nodded weakly. "It feels like the worst hangover ever, but obviously I haven't gotten drunk lately."

"Okay, follow me." She led him to the lounge and its couch. "If you want to rest here, I'll go get you some herbs." She looked up at him. "Unless you'd be more comfortable in your room? We could go there instead."

He shook his head, maybe too quickly. He wanted her help, wanted her company, but didn't think they should be alone in his *bedroom* together. That seemed a little too risky. He collapsed on the couch. "This will be fine."

"May I touch your forehead?"

He nodded.

Her hand felt cool, light, magnificent. When she pulled her hand away, he wished she'd put it back.

"You definitely have a fever. That's good."

"That's good? Aakesh tried to kill me. Do you know he made me beat myself with a tree?"

She giggled, a sound he found quite rewarding. "You're experiencing detox symptoms, and the fever means your body is expelling toxins. Trust me. This is all really good news. I'll tell you more about it if you're interested"—he really wasn't—"but right now I want to help you feel better, so what are your other symptoms? Do you feel sick to your stomach?"

"No," he said, realizing how grateful he was that he *didn't* feel as though he was going to throw up. "I only feel really weak and dizzy, and my head is pounding."

"Okay. I'll be right back. You rest. You want a blanket?"

He nodded. It felt so good to be taken care of by her. When was the last time someone had taken care of him? His mother? When he was a kid? Heidi disappeared, and he missed her. But he felt much better in this dimly lit room that smelled of ginger, with this soft blanket pulled up to his chin. He was never going into a sauna again. He didn't know if he even believed in this detox quackery, but if his body had toxins in it, he would just as soon keep them there, thank you very much.

He felt himself drifting toward sleep and fought it. He wanted to sleep, but if she came back and found him asleep, she'd probably let him sleep, and he didn't want that to happen. He'd rather live with the headache and get to spend more time with her. This realization made his stomach roll. What was wrong with him? He had to stop this. There was no future with this woman. He shouldn't be getting attached. But what if there *was* a future with her? Couldn't she be a health coach in Boston? There were lots of unhealthy people there. And there was a park. She could go commune with the birds and trees there, couldn't she? Though they didn't have giant, steroidally enhanced mosquitos in Boston. At least, not that he'd met.

She returned with a mug.

He sat up halfway. "What's in that?"

She smiled. "Do you really want to know?"

She handed him the mug, which was hot enough to burn his hands, but he tried to hide the fact that she'd just scalded him. He quickly grabbed the handle and blew on the greenish liquid in his cup. There was brown stuff swirling around on top, and it smelled pungent. "You're right. I don't want to know."

She pulled something out of her pocket. "I also brought some peppermint and frankincense oil. I'd like to apply it to your head if you're comfortable with that."

*Oh yes, I am quite comfortable with the idea of you putting your fingers on my forehead again.* He nodded. "Sure."

She perched on the edge of the couch, a position he thought must have been uncomfortable. He scooted back to make more room for her, and she slid closer. "Where does it hurt, exactly?"

He didn't know. "It's hard to pinpoint. Everywhere? It's like radiating out from the center. It feels like my head is going to pop off, like a little kid's playing with a dandelion, and my head is the blossom that's about to be sacrificed."

She smiled as she tapped some oil out onto her hands. "You have a way with words." She rubbed her hands together. "But that does make sense, and sounds like a detox headache." She placed her gloriously cool fingers on his temples, and he lay back to make the job easier for her.

*This feels like heaven.* She moved her fingertips into his hair and massaged the oil into his scalp, and this felt even better than heaven. He didn't want her to stop. Ever. It was almost worth the headache.

"Is that frankincense? All I can smell is mint."

"This is only the peppermint. I thought I'd save the frankincense for your feet."

*My feet?!* Oh no! His feet were impossibly ticklish. He couldn't let her touch them. He would laugh like a hyena and embarrass himself beyond recovery.

"Is that okay?" she asked.

He didn't know what to say. He closed his eyes, hoping the scenario would go away.

"You looked nervous. Do you not like it when people touch your feet?"

"What?" He squeezed his eyes shut tighter.

She stopped rubbing. "It's okay. Some people don't like having their feet—"

"No, it's okay," he blurted out. She was going to think he was a freak—afraid of having his feet touched.

"Oh good." She slid down the couch. "I'm not trying to get fresh ..."

Get fresh? Who used that phrase anymore? She reminded him of his grandmother. At that thought, a warm feeling filled his chest. She slipped off his flip-flops and was still jabbering on about frankincense.

"I'm sorry, what?"

"Is your mind feeling a bit foggy? You're acting a little different."

"Oh, I'm foggy all right. What were you saying?"

She grabbed the top of his foot with one hand and he jerked, but only a little. She didn't seem to notice. She then let go to put some oil on her hand.

"I was saying that every nerve line in your body ends in your feet"—he didn't believe this for a second. She was *such* a quack. But she was a cute, sweet quack who smelled like flowers—"and lastly, the pores in your feet are bigger than elsewhere in your body, so they absorb the oil better." Okay, that part might be true.

Here it came, the moment of truth. He held his breath and bore down as her gentle fingers touched the arch of his foot.

But it was no use. Against his will, his knee jerked up, yanking his foot from her grasp, as a hyena howl erupted from his throat. He opened one eye to see her expression, wishing he could wipe the idiot smile off his face. It was crazy to be smiling like that when his head hurt as badly as it did. His hyena howl had doubled his head pain.

She raised an eyebrow. "Ticklish much?"

Oh good. She was amused.

"You know what? I'm feeling much better now. I think the peppermint did the trick."

She held out one hand. "Give me your foot back."

"I don't think that's such a good idea."

"Give it to me." She reached for it, grabbed it with a firm hand, and yanked it back to her lap. "If you'd *told* me you were ticklish, I would have been less gentle."

"I don't think it's going to matt—" He shrieked again. *Good grief, could this get any more embarrassing?*

She rubbed even harder, and, though it still tickled, it was tolerable. She finished with his right foot and reached for his left. "Is this one less ticklish?"

"More," he cried, mortified.

"Okay, here goes," she warned, and then she was rubbing again, and he was giggling again, like a high school cheerleader with a crush. His eyes were squeezed shut, and tears leaked out the corners of them.

"There you go." She removed her hands. "That should help. Now drink your tea and try to get some rest."

## 12

Heidi waited until the safety of the staff bathroom before she let herself laugh at Chad and his ticklishness. What a baby! How much she had wanted to tickle his feet till he begged for mercy, but alas, she was a professional. Sort of.

She finished washing her hands and then headed for the kitchen. She had to discuss Gloria the dancer's nutritional needs with Bob. She found him making zucchini noodles.

"Zucchini?" she said. "That didn't come from our garden. At least, not yet."

"No. They came from afar," he admitted. "I bought them at the grocery store. I'm trying to come up with something Chad will enjoy. He wasn't very excited with the Spicy Asian Salad he had for lunch."

She scrunched up her nose. "Is that the one with all the onions in it?"

"Yes, ma'am. So, I'm making him some ravioli."

"You're giving him cheese?" She couldn't believe it.

"You know me better than that. No, I made some raw cashew butter, with nutritional yeast for that cheesy-like flavor."

"Oh wow! Can you put some parsley in the sauce? He needs more parsley."

"Absolutely. I was already planning on it."

She bent to sniff the bowl of filling. "Smells delicious. I hope he doesn't like it, so I can have some."

"Oh, don't worry. I'm going to make enough for everyone."

"Seriously? That's going to take you forever." She watched him spoon some of his filling onto a zucchini noodle and begin to fold it into a square.

"You want to help?"

She really didn't, but she knew that if the roles were reversed, Bob would totally help her fold zucchini. So she dragged a stool over to his side of the island and settled in. He showed her what to do, and after two failed attempts, which she set aside to eat later, she got the knack of it. *Yes,* she thought, *Chad* will *like these.*

"You like him, don't you?" Bob said.

"Who?"

"Don't play dumb with me. You're smiling at your zucchini. The billionaire. You like the billionaire."

"Money means nothing to me, Bob. I don't like him because he's a billionaire."

"Aha!" Bob cried. "So you *do* like him."

She felt flustered. "That's not what I meant. Don't try to trick me. I think he's a very interesting person, but I'm not interested in him romantically."

"Sure." Bob couldn't have sounded less sure. "I see the way you look at him, with gaga eyes. I've never seen you look at anyone like that before. And we've had some handsome men come through here. Even some rich ones. This guy's different."

Heidi took a deep breath and looked at Bob. Her hands kept folding.

"Pay attention!" he cried, pointing at her latest square, which was now more of a rhombus.

"Sorry," she said, and tried to focus.

"It's okay. Now, you were saying?"

"I wasn't saying anything," she said.

"You were about to tell me all the details about your crush on the billionaire."

"Oh, will you stop calling him that?"

"Why? If you don't have feelings for him, why do you care what I call him?"

"For heaven's sake! Fine. I do like him a little. But *only* a little. And it totally doesn't matter, because he lives in the fast lane, and I have no desire to live in the fast lane. And he lives in Boston. And he is rich, and I don't even like money."

"You know, I've been a bohemian for a while now. And I know it's very cool to say that we don't like money. But as I've grown older, I've also realized it's pretty silly."

"What?" Heidi couldn't believe what he'd just said.

"I get that you don't like greed and corruption, but that's not money's fault. And money can help people. Money is what allows people to come here and get better. Money can help you have fun and enjoy life. I'm not saying you're wrong, but maybe reconsider your views. It might be awesome to date a billionaire. He's probably got a bowling alley in his basement."

His argument made some sense, except for maybe the bowling alley part, but Heidi wasn't completely swayed. "Okay, forget about the money issue then. He is a *client*, and I am therefore *forbidden* from having a romantic relationship with him."

"By who?"

"What?" She set another ravioli on his tray. This one had come out perfectly. Confessing truth made her ninety-degree angles much sharper.

"Who has forbidden you from having a relationship with a client?"

"What? You're not even making sense now. Common sense forbids it! Professional ethics. And I don't think my *boss* would be too happy with the idea either."

Bob began peeling another zucchini. "Don't use Naihma as an excuse. She's not your typical boss, and you know it. She just wants you to be happy and healthy. She wants the same for Chad. So if the happiest and healthiest you two can be involves being together, then she would be all for it."

"You sound pretty sure of yourself. You ever had a crush on a client?"

He laughed. "How do you think I met my wife?"

"You're kidding!" Heidi knew all about Bob's wonderful marriage. They were the epitome of matrimonial bliss. But she'd never heard how they met.

"It's true. We were both guests here, many moons ago. I was trying to kick a bad habit. She was trying to heal from an abusive relationship. We met in the herb garden, just like in a good beatnik poem." He chuckled. "And the rest is history, as they say."

She could feel his eyes on her.

"I'm just saying, never say never. You have no idea what fate has in store for you."

"I'm happy with the life I have."

"I get that. But you could be even happier with the life you could have."

"A-huh." She waited for him to say more, but he didn't. So she concentrated on folding the thinly sliced vegetable. And the more she folded, the more zucchini he sliced. She thought she had folded approximately seven thousand ravioli and was wondering what army they were planning to feed, when Bob announced they were out of zucchini.

"Thank goodness," Heidi said as she finished folding her last one. "My fingers are cramping."

"Oh stop it. Our clients pay good money for this food. I want to give them the best."

"I know you do. And I'm the same way. I want to give my *clients* my best too, which means not getting distracted by foolishness."

Bob gave her an understanding look, but she thought she saw some sadness in his eyes too.

"And this is the kitchen!" Naihma declared, showing a tall woman into the room.

And there she was. Gloria in all her glory. And she was *gorgeous.* Long dark hair piled atop a heart-shaped face. Her eyes were bright blue, and her cheeks perfectly pink. The body of a supermodel.

As Naihma made the introductions, and Heidi gave Gloria her best welcome smile, Chad walked in right behind them.

## 13

Chad couldn't believe how bad he felt. Whatever Heidi had done to him with the oils had helped, but the effects were wearing off. He tried to walk around the two women blocking the entryway to the kitchen in order to get to Heidi.

"Chad!" Naihma said, her boisterous voice sending sharp knives through this skull. "This is our new guest, Gloria Davison, from Boston."

"We've met!" Gloria declared. She batted her eyelashes at him.

*We have?* Maybe, maybe not. He was in no condition to remember anyone. In his current condition of fog-brain, he could've done the foxtrot with the pope for all he knew.

"So nice to see you again, Chad!" She stepped forward to embrace him, and he flinched at her touch. He had no idea who this woman was and he was embarrassed by the amount of sweat clinging to his skin and clothes.

The woman released him, and he looked at Heidi. "I think I'm getting worse. Can I have some more tea?"

"What's going on?" Bob asked, and Chad was touched by his concern.

Chad collapsed onto a stool.

"Chad here is having some detox symptoms," Heidi explained.

"Oh!" Bob looked at Heidi. "Should we slow it down?"

"Slow what down?" Chad didn't like the sound of this.

"Slow the detox down," Heidi explained.

"Yes, why don't you?" Naihma said.

"Because we've only got Chad for a week," Heidi said. She put her hands on her hips. It was adorable. "We want him to get better, not slow his healing down."

"I understand, but we also don't want him to be miserable while he's on vacation." Naihma's voice was sterner than Chad had ever heard it.

"What are you detoxing from?" Gloria cooed, but everyone ignored her. Chad thought he saw Heidi give her a dirty look, but his vision was a bit blurry.

"How do we slow it down?" Chad asked, his voice barely audible.

"I'll prepare you some steamed veggies," Bob said.

*Yuck!* Could he steam him a cheeseburger instead? "I thought you didn't have a stove."

"We don't," Bob said, "but I keep a hot plate under lock and key for such an occasion as this. You won't be the first one we've had to break it out for. Going all raw can be quite a shock to the system, especially with Heidi's herbs at work."

Chad couldn't believe steamed veggies would help. "That's it? Eat some cooked vegetables?"

Bob nodded. "That's it. It will relieve your symptoms, but, as Heidi said, it will slow down your healing a bit."

"Get him some green beans," Naihma said.

Heidi, hands still on hips, said, "How about we let Chad choose? Chad, do you want to push through and get to the other side quicker? Or do you want to slow down your healing for a quick fix?"

"Heidi!" Naihma scolded. "That's not a fair way to present his choices." Naihma drew closer to him. "Chad, don't let her pressure you. She can be a bit overzealous sometimes." She gave Heidi a harsh look. "It's because she's passionate about healing, but don't let her—"

"I'll do it," Chad managed, his voice a hoarse whisper. He didn't know if his body was capable of producing adrenaline in that moment, but it was trying. Every cell in his being wanted to defend Heidi, to defend her methods, to keep her from getting in trouble for trying to help him. Even if that meant he might die in the process. "I'll do it," he said again, with a smidge more oomph this time. "I want to get better. I just came in here for more tea." He looked at Heidi then, and the affection he believed he saw in her eyes made all his pain and suffering worth it, even if he did die of detox. At least, he *thought* it was affection. It could have been the fever talking.

"Can you get to your room?" Heidi asked.

He nodded.

"Great. Take your time. I'll meet you there with tea and oil."

"Thank you," he croaked and turned to go.

He traveled at the pace of a lazy turtle, keeping one hand on the wall just in case, and was almost to his room when he smelled perfume behind him. The scent of it made his stomach roll, and he hoped against hope he didn't barf in Serenity Hills' hallway.

"I can't believe you don't remember me," she said. Her voice was smooth, sophisticated.

He stopped walking, but he didn't turn around.

"Don't you remember that party? We dined and danced, drank wine and laughed till midnight!"

*Can she not see that I'm dying here? And maybe not in the mood for chitchat?*

She stepped in front of him. "It was a benefit dinner."

He couldn't remember going to a benefit dinner. Ever.

"It's okay if you don't remember." She leaned closer, making her perfume much more unbearable, and lowered her voice. "Like I said, there was a lot of wine involved." She tipped her head back and tittered.

The thought of wine made his stomach roll again. A buzzing sensation went through his head, and he closed his eyes to staunch it, but it only made it worse. This was it. He was really going to pass out. He, a grown man, was going to faint in the hall, mere feet from his room, right in front of this beautiful woman. But on the heels of that thought came the realization that he was beyond caring. He felt his legs fold, groped for the wall beside him, and felt the woman's arms go around him. She squeezed her arms around his chest and held him up. She was stronger than she looked. He was desperately trying to get his feet back under him, when he heard a familiar voice.

"What is going on here?"

## 14

Heidi came around the corner, a cup of hot tea in hand, to find Chad and Gloria in a tight embrace. Her first instinct was a jealous rage with a hint of betrayal, but then she saw that Chad's legs weren't quite straight.

She put the tea down on the floor and rushed to his aid.

"I'm okay, I'm okay," he said. "Just a little dizzy."

Heidi pulled one of his arms out of the Chad-Gloria tangle, and put it around her shoulder. She hated to ask Gloria for help, hated to even have to *speak* to Gloria, but—desperate times. "Can you help me get him into his bedroom?"

"Certainly," Gloria said.

Heidi thought she heard some innuendo there. *Stop it. Focus on the task at hand, not the foolishness going on inside your own head.*

They got him into the room and onto his bed.

"Thanks, ladies. You're the best." He sounded a little drunk.

"We should let him rest," Heidi said as she gave Gloria what she hoped was a strong look.

"All right. See you around, AgriChoice." And with more grace than necessary or decent, she left the room.

Heidi looked down at his closed eyes. "AgriChoice?"

"It's the name of my company."

"Oh. I like it. It's poetic. Hang on." She hurried out into the hallway to retrieve the tea, wondering about Gloria's and Chad's relationship. Did they really know each other? But he hadn't recognized her picture when he'd seen it on the computer monitor. Of course, he hadn't gotten a good look at it either.

With care, she brought the tea into his bedroom. "Here's your tea. But I'm also going to get you some cooked veggies." She set the tea on his nightstand. "I'm sorry, Chad. Naihma is right. Sometimes I *am* overzealous. I'm only trying to help, but I don't want to torture you." She turned to go, but he grabbed her hand.

When she turned back to look at him, his eyes were open. He relaxed his grip on her wrist, and she was glad he didn't let go completely. His touch sent shivers up her spine.

"Will I feel better in the morning?"

She nodded. "You're going to feel like a million bucks."

He gave her a lopsided smile that reminded her of a floppy-eared bunny she'd had as a kid. Georgie. One of his ears had always been crooked. Golly how she'd loved that bunny.

"I don't want to slow down the healing," he said. "I trust you."

She didn't know what to say. Why on earth did he trust her? He'd only known her for one day, and so far, the evidence wasn't pointing in her favor.

"Can I have some more peppermint oil? You can skip the feet this time." He tried to smile again.

"Of course." She pulled the oil out of her pocket and dabbed some onto her fingertips.

"I just want to sleep. That's all. You promised you'd help me sleep, and I think you have. If I don't fall asleep in the next ten minutes, I'll eat my hat."

She rubbed his temples. "Are you still dizzy?"

"No, I'm feeling much better now that I'm lying down, away from all the lights and strong smells."

Heidi furrowed her brow. "What strong smells?"

He snickered. "Never mind. They're gone now."

She took her hands away from his head. "Okay. Is there anything else I can do for you?"

"No. But thank you. Tomorrow will be a

brand-new day. Let's run a marathon. Maybe swim the Bering Strait. Or compete in a Taekwondo tournament."

She giggled. "Go to sleep. If you do need anything, or change your mind about the cooked green beans, find someone who will find me."

He rolled onto his side and curled into the fetal position. She had an urge to curl up next to him, but shook it out of her head.

"I rarely change my mind about anything," he said, his eyes closed.

She gently shut the door and headed back to the kitchen, where she found Naihma, Bob, and Gloria dining on the ravioli she had so painstakingly crafted for Chad. She resented them for eating them so quickly, without even appreciating their art. *Well, I probably shouldn't resent Bob for that*, she thought, *as he did much more of the work than I did.*

Naihma looked up when she approached. "How is he?"

"A little better, I think."

"What's wrong with him?" Gloria asked, not even trying to hide the accusation in her voice. She clearly believed Heidi had done something sinister to him.

"We serve a living food diet here," Bob said, coming to Heidi's rescue. "He's had nothing but raw fruits and veggies since he got here, so his body is getting rid of some of the junk it's been storing. It can make you feel pretty yucky."

"Oh!" Gloria dabbed at her perfectly clean lips with a napkin. "That won't happen to me. I already eat a vegan diet."

Heidi rolled her eyes at Bob and then hoped Naihma hadn't seen it. *I have to get a grip.*

"Would you like some food?" Bob asked Heidi, already getting up before she answered.

"Oh gosh, yes." She wasn't usually an emotional eater, but again—desperate times. She sat down at the table across from Gloria.

"So, I was just telling them about Chad!" Gloria said. "We know each other back in Boston!"

*Oh boy.* Heidi averted her eyes by trying to scrape an imaginary spot off the table with her fingernail.

"We've been to benefit dinners together."
*As in on dates?*

"He is *such* a generous philanthropist. He's given away *millions* of dollars. To youth programs, orphanages in Africa, churches ..."

Heidi tried to stop listening. She didn't like the idea of Gloria knowing so much about him. And she wasn't sure she wanted to hear more awesome stuff about him. It was hard enough ignoring her feelings when she thought he was a rich snob. But a rich snob who gave millions of dollars away to children in need? That was a whole different ball game.

Bob slid a plateful of zucchini ravioli in front of her, and she dug in. As Gloria prattled on, Heidi decided that Chad wasn't the only one who would go to bed early that night.

## 15

Chad woke to the sound of birdsong out his window. He had opened his window upon Heidi's advice—"Fresh air cures everything," she'd said—and now it sounded as though he was lying in a crowded aviary.

He sat up. When he'd told Heidi that today would be a brand-new day, he'd said it with his tongue in his cheek. But maybe he shouldn't have. He'd never felt so good in his life. He stood up and weight-tested his legs to make sure they were back to normal. They felt as if they'd never betrayed him before. He stood on one foot. Then the other. All systems go.

He desperately wanted a shower, but first— yerba maté. No use ruining this glorious mood with a caffeine headache. He resisted the urge to skip down the hall toward the kitchen, and when he got there, he was disappointed to find it empty. Of course, he'd been hoping to see Heidi—not because he was romantically interested in her or anything, but because he wanted to tell her how much better he was feeling. His desire to see her was all business. But he had also been hoping to see Bob, or anyone. For the first time that he could remember—ever—he was in the mood for human interaction.

But, Heidi had told him, solitude is also

healthy, and so he tried to enjoy the peace and quiet as he spooned out the Argentinian leaves and twigs.

His solitude was soon interrupted by Fawsa. "Good morning, Chad!"

"Good morning," he said, and actually meant it. He hardly used the expression, and when he did, he didn't ever mean it.

"I try not to harass our guests. I don't want to pressure anyone into talking to me, but I want to make sure you know that my door is always open."

"Okay." Normally, this conversation would have annoyed him, but not this morning.

"Do you know where my office is?"

"Sure do!" He had no idea.

"Okay, so maybe we'll see you there later? No pressure."

"Sure, maybe!"

She stared at him for a few seconds and then left the room. He thought that, if he *wanted* to talk about his feelings, which he didn't, but if he *did*, he would rather talk to Heidi.

He took his beverage through the sliding glass doors and into the backyard, which seemed to be mostly gardens. They were beautiful. *When have I ever thought a garden was beautiful?* He almost laughed at himself. A wooden porch swing hung from a stand, and he sat down, pushed off with his toes, and enjoyed the feel of the small breeze on his face as he waited for his caffeine to steep.

He began to marvel at the busy bees flying all over the garden, flitting from flower to flower. There were so many of them, yet they never seemed to get in one another's way. And weren't they all business! A model of efficiency. He began to feel guilty about his own business back home. He didn't see these bees taking vacations, detoxing, or sitting around in a garden drinking hippie tea. No, they were industrious. They were taking care of business. Not letting anything—or anyone—distract them from their goals.

He didn't even hear Heidi approaching, but suddenly she stood beside him. "How are you feeling?"

He smiled up at her, and the sunshine made the eye closest to her squint, which he feared looked like a wink. He quickly looked down at his tea. "Better. Good actually. No headache. No dizziness. No fever. Good as new. And it's only Tuesday. So maybe I don't have to stay for the whole week." He really hoped she hadn't just thought he was winking at her. Even though she did seem to have a habit of winking at him. He wondered if she winked at everyone.

She sat down beside him. She smelled like

lilacs. "You're not enjoying your stay?"

"It's not that," he rushed to say. "I'm missing *so much* back home. The guy I've got running things is very good at what he does, but he's not me, and he doesn't have the vested interest in my company that I do. I just like to be at the helm. And I'm feeling so much better. I think I'm really ready." He held out his arm to her. "Go ahead, take my blood pressure."

She smiled, but it looked like a sad smile. "We can do that later. I don't have my blood pressure cuff with me. The longer you stay, the more you'll heal, and the stronger you'll be when you get back to work. Isn't your business worth that?"

"Sure. But can't I continue this stuff at home? You know, drink juice, eat herbs, breathe fresh air, and drink gross tea?"

She giggled. "You *could.* But *would you*?"

"I will." He would try at least.

Heidi looked out at the garden. "Gloria was regaling us last night with tales of your philanthropy. You are really quite generous."

"My what?" What was she talking about?

Heidi looked at him. "Philanthropy. As in giving money away."

"I know what the word means. I just don't know what Gloria told you."

"Oh, it was pretty impressive. How you've adopted three elephants in Asia. How you built an orphanage in Uganda. How you financed a youth recreational center in Boston."

*What? Where was all this coming from?*

"She went on and on. Pretty amazing stuff."

*Elephants?!* "Yeah. Pretty amazing, all right."

"You don't sound proud."

"Uh …" He had no idea what to say. Why would Gloria spread such lies about him?

"Sorry, didn't mean to embarrass you. I was just really impressed. I don't know. I guess I owe you an apology. I thought that since you were so rich, you must be greedy too." She flashed him a quick smile. "I always think, if someone has a lot of money, they must have gotten it by taking advantage of others. But with you, at least, that's not true. So, I'm sorry I made such assumptions. Can you forgive me?"

He looked down at the ground. "Uh, yeah. Sure."

"Great!" She jumped up. "I'm meeting Gloria at the yoga hut. Would you like to join us?"

He didn't want to join them. He thought yoga was ridiculous. He had no idea how to do it, and he didn't want to try. Certainly not in front of Heidi. But his lips seemed to have a mind of their own. "Sure. Sounds great. I'll meet you there."

## 16

There were few things in the world Heidi loved more than yoga. She had personally seen yoga cure a myriad of health issues, and she was excited to introduce Chad to this ancient practice. She was less excited about leading Gloria through a session, but Gloria's hamstring really needed some TLC, and Heidi, at her core, was about helping people heal— even people who annoyed her a little. Or a lot.

"Aren't we going to go inside?" Gloria asked, nodding at the small building designated for yoga.

"No, fresh air is so good for us. We only use the building when the weather isn't cooperating."

"People come here in the *winter*?" Chad appeared incredulous.

"It's beautiful here in the winter," Heidi said. "And the sauna to brook run is twice as fun."

"You're kidding," Chad said. "People do that in the *winter*?"

"Well, Aakesh does anyway. We also go snowshoeing and cross-country skiing. You should come back then and check it out." Her cheeks grew hot. She hadn't meant to sound as though she were begging him to come back.

*It might be best if I just get on with the show,*

she thought. "First, we're going to sit and rest for a few minutes." She sat on the ground and crossed her legs. "Criss-cross applesauce. Just like in preschool."

"I don't remember preschool," Chad mumbled, but he sat down.

Gloria tittered as if he'd said something witty. Then she looked at the ground as if it was contagious. "We're not going to use mats?"

"Not today. I like to have people connect their skin to the earth. I think it's good for grounding them. Try it. You'll see."

Gloria didn't look convinced, but she joined them in the grass.

Heidi took a deep breath. *She gets on my last nerve. It's a good thing I'm about to do yoga.* "Okay. Now close your eyes, and focus on your breathing. Try to bring in as much air as you can and then let it out slowly. Then, when you think you've got it all out, push a little more, and I bet you'll get some more air out. Then you're ready to refuel."

She took several deep breaths and resisted the urge to open her eyes and watch Chad breathe. Not only should she not even have such a desire, but she figured that's what Gloria was doing, and Heidi didn't want to get caught doing the same.

"Now try to check in with your body. What

feels good today? What is tight? What is sore? Just spend a minute taking a survey of your physical self." She gave them time. "Okay, you can open your eyes if you want. The first pose I want to show you is called the child's pose." She demonstrated and then she looked up to see how they were coming with their own poses. "This is a good one for reducing stress, and most people can do it. So if you're ever in a yoga session and people are doing something too advanced for you, you can always just do this pose. It's like taking a break, but it's not a break because you're still doing yoga." They each seemed to be doing fine with it, so Heidi put her head back down. "Now continue your deep breathing. Mmm. Smell that rich earth beneath your nose. We're going to hold this for seven more deep breaths. So ... in ... and out ... in ... and out." Several breaths later, she said, "Okay, now carefully turn over onto your back. And we're going to try to make our bodies as long as possible. Reach as far as you can with your fingertips and as far in the other direction with your toes. Feel your spine stretch out like a string."

"This is like second grade yoga," Gloria said. "We *are* going to get more advanced, right?"

After a moment of internal debate, Heidi chose not to answer her. "And take three more deep breaths." She waited for more heckling from the peanut gallery, but the heckler gave her a break.

"Now, pull your knees to your chest, and wrap your arms around your shins. Gently pull your shins to your chest, but keep breathing."

It sounded like a tiny, high-pitched trumpet. Heidi had heard plenty of people accidentally pass gas during yoga—it was almost par for the course—but this didn't sound like that. This sounded like a child trying to blow into a ram's horn for the first time, and not giving it enough air. For several seconds, Heidi didn't even know what she'd heard. She wondered if there was a wild animal nearby, but couldn't figure out what kind of animal would make a noise like that.

She did recognize the noise that followed. It sounded like a fifth grade boy's snicker. And she knew it had come from Chad.

Realization dawned. She tried to move on, and, as she always did in similar situations, pretend nothing had happened. Which would have been so much easier if Chad hadn't giggled. "Now, still holding on to your knees, gently rock back and forth. Let the ground give you a backrub."

"This is ridiculous. Grass is stabbing into my back." And then, as if she did it on purpose, as if her digestive system was trying to punctuate her verbal point, it happened again. The same little trumpet squeak. And this time, Chad let out more than a giggle.

"Well, I never ..." Gloria jumped up, showing no signs of an injured hamstring, and said, "You two should be ashamed of yourselves!"

*Me? What did I do? I just work here!*

Chad let go of his legs, and they flopped forward onto the ground like pool noodles. "I'm sorry, Gloria. You're right. I'm being childish. I'm just in a bizarrely good mood. I feel silly."

Gloria looked down at him, her face red, her body trembling, and said, "How dare you treat me like this? I'm so out of here." And she stormed off.

Heidi watched her go, wondering what she should do, what she *could* do to rectify the situation.

Chad didn't even wait until she was out of earshot before laughing. And he *really* laughed this time. He held his stomach with one hand, and his whole chest shook with it.

Heidi couldn't help it. Laughter was contagious. She began to laugh too.

This made Chad laugh harder. "Can you imagine?" he squeaked out between throes of laughter.

"Imagine what?"

He turned his head to look at her, and she saw tears rolling down his face. "Can you imagine ... if we had done the advanced poses ..." He spoke the last two words with as much sarcasm as he could muster given how hard he was laughing. "Imagine what noise would have come out of her!" Then he rolled his whole body onto its side, so he was facing Heidi. "It would've sounded like a marching band's entire horn section!" He let out another bark of laughter and flopped back over onto his back.

Heidi let him laugh. She didn't know what else to do, and she figured laughter was good for the soul, even if it was at Gloria's expense. And besides, seeing Chad happy made her happy. It wasn't lost on her that she wasn't usually so connected to her clients' emotional states.

## 17

The last thing Chad wanted to do was apologize to Gloria, but he knew it was the right thing to do. So he set out to find her, but he had no idea where she was.

He hadn't meant to be so harsh. That wasn't like him. He usually had more control over his emotions. If he was honest with himself, he really had no idea what was going on right now. It was as if he had found a whole new version of himself.

He wandered all over the property looking, but he didn't see her. He headed inside. She wasn't in the kitchen. Or the library or the lounge. He didn't want to go looking for her room, so he looked around for a staff member to ask. The first person he found was Bob, which was good, because after Heidi, Bob was his favorite person at Serenity Hills. Not only did Bob feed Chad, which was important, but Bob was almost normal.

"Hey, Bob! What's cooking?"

Bob looked up from the carrots he was chopping. "Is that a joke?"

"Yeah, it was sort of supposed to be. Was it not funny?"

"Yeah, sure it was funny. I just wanted to make sure you weren't for real. Now, are you hungry? I've got some scrumptious beet juice in the fridge."

Chad shuddered at the thought. "No thanks. I came in here to ask you if you knew where Gloria was."

The look on Bob's face was difficult to read. Was he sad? Disgusted? Confused? Whatever the emotion was, it wasn't joy at the sound of her name. Chad wondered if Bob didn't like Gloria. He'd already gotten the impression that Heidi didn't. Maybe none of the Serenity Hills staff liked her. Maybe they knew something about her that he didn't know.

"No. Sorry, I haven't seen her."

"Is something wrong, Bob?"

"No. Sorry, I was being nosy and wondering why you were looking for Gloria."

"I'm embarrassed to explain—"

"Then of course you don't have to!"

"No, it's okay. It's just karma at work." *Did I just use the word karma? What are these people doing to me?* "I might have poked a little fun at her during yoga. So I wanted to apologize."

"Well, in that case. I suppose you should be looking for her. I was … well, as I said, I was being nosy. I can't help but notice that you and Heidi seem to be awfully compatible. So, when you said you were looking for Gloria, I was worried you might be pursuing the wrong woman."

Chad wasn't sure what to say to this. He hadn't expected this explanation. "I'm not *pursuing* anyone. Heidi does seem like a fascinating woman, and I do very much enjoy being around her, and I'm very grateful for what she has done to help me get healthier. But, really, there is nothing else between us. I mean, come on, I live four hours away, and that's with no traffic. How often is there no traffic between here and Boston?"

"There's very little traffic on this end." Bob smirked.

"You know what I mean. Besides, we are from two very different worlds. I like life in the fast lane, and she likes life ... well ... *here.*"

"Is here so bad? It seems to be growing on you."

Chad looked around the kitchen with fondness. "You're right, Bob. I was so certain that I was going to hate this place, I wasn't even going to give it a chance. But it certainly has its merits. I'm feeling better than I've ever felt, or at least that I can ever remember feeling. But I still couldn't live here."

"If you say so, but like I said to Heidi, never say never."

Chad jerked his eyes back to Bob. "What do you mean, what you said to Heidi? You've discussed this with Heidi?" He found the idea extraordinarily embarrassing.

"Nope, no discussion really. Our conversation was a lot like this one. She denied the chemistry between you, and I told her to never say never." Bob shrugged and went back to chopping. "That's it."

Chad wanted to ask him if he thought that Heidi had feelings for him, but that felt a bit too much like how one would behave in high school. He stood there for an awkward minute watching Bob chop, trying to think of a non-high school question to ask, but came up blank. "All right then. Thanks for your help."

Bob looked up, and there was kindness in his eyes. "I don't think I was much help, but if you can think of a way that I could be helpful, please come back and let me know."

"Sure thing." Chad left the kitchen with his mind spinning. Is this what Serenity Hills staff did in their spare time? Played matchmaker with the clients?

Chad resumed his search for Gloria, and soon found her. She was lying in a hammock, and he wasn't sure if she was awake. He approached slowly, but then he saw that her eyes were open and didn't want to sneak up on her so he called out. "Hey, dancer." Why had he called her that? He didn't know. He was trying to be nice. Maybe he wasn't very good at nice. It felt awkward, like shoes that didn't quite fit.

She looked up. "Hi, AgriChoice."

He sure didn't like being called that. Especially by her. "I owe you an apology."

"I'd really rather not talk about it." She closed her eyes. "I'm quite embarrassed."

"Oh, don't be. Please. These things happen. Life happens. Am I right? And what happens at Serenity Hills stays at Serenity Hills." He was laying on the charm as thickly as he could, but he had never been confident that he was terribly charming. Whether or not he was charming, she was not responding. She looked like her dog had just died. "Are you all right?"

She kept her eyes pinched shut. "Of course I'm not all right. I'm ashamed, and I can't wait to get out of here." She folded her arms across her chest dramatically.

"Ashamed? Don't you think that's a strong term? It really wasn't any big deal."

"Any big deal?" she cried. "Maybe not to you, but this is my life we're talking about!" She gracefully rolled out of the hammock, landed like a cat, and then departed in a hurry.

He had absolutely no idea what had just happened. That was the worst apology in the history of apologies. Somehow, he had managed to make things worse. But he was also beyond caring. He had no idea why she had gotten so upset, but he also didn't want to figure it out. He was tired of dealing with emotions and emotional people. He never did these things, and his stamina for such activities was low. He had tried with Gloria and he had failed, but that was okay. He wouldn't be there much longer, and he decided to spend the rest of his time trying to avoid Gloria and trying to avoid offending her.

## 18

Heidi knew she had to apologize to Gloria. Even though Chad had been mostly to blame, Heidi was supposed to be the professional. She didn't think that Gloria would tattle on her to Naihma, but one could never be too sure. She had seen Gloria in the hammock earlier, but she had appeared to be sleeping, and Heidi hadn't wanted to wake her up. Not only did Gloria need her rest if she was going to heal, but waking people up often made them cranky, and if Heidi wanted her to accept an apology, then cranky mode probably wasn't the best starting point.

Later, when Heidi went looking for her, she couldn't find her anywhere. She went into the kitchen. Bob was making avocado pudding. "That looks yummy! Have you seen Gloria?"

"Why is everybody looking for Gloria?" As soon as he spoke the words, he cringed. It was clear he regretted asking the question.

"What does that mean? Who else has been looking for her?" Heidi heard her own voice go up an octave, and was glad only Bob was there to hear her squeaking.

"Never mind. I was just babbling."

"No, tell me." She tried to keep her voice at a reasonable pitch. "Was it Chad?"

"Are you jealous?" Bob smirked.

"No, of course not. It's ... we both sort of offended her today, and I was looking for her so that I could apologize, and I was wondering if he already had."

Bob let out a puff of air. "Yes, it was Chad. He was in here earlier looking for her. He said he had to apologize. But I didn't know where she was then, and I don't know where she is now. I do know that her presence has brought a lot of drama to our little home here."

"Isn't that the truth?" She started to leave, but then turned back around. "Did you and Chad talk about anything else?"

Bob gave her a mischievous smile. "Wouldn't you like to know?"

Heidi knew Bob well enough to know that: yes, they had talked about something else; and no, Bob was not going to share the details with her. So she gave up and left.

She finally found Gloria sitting by the brook, splashing her feet in the water. Heidi couldn't help but notice that her toenails were perfectly pedicured, with purple polish. The sparkles in the polish reflected the sunlight. Heidi grimaced.

"Hey, Gloria!" Heidi tried to sound perky and friendly. "May I join you?"

Gloria shrugged. "I don't own this riverbank."

Heidi resisted the urge to tell this city slicker that the tiny slope they were sitting on was most certainly not a riverbank. Not even close. She sat down beside her—but not too close. "I wanted to apologize for earlier. And I wanted to tell you, that sort of stuff happens in nearly every yoga session we have here."

She stopped kicking and looked at Heidi. "Then why did you laugh?"

"That's why I'm apologizing. I laughed because Chad laughed, and I'm afraid that laughter is contagious, but really, please don't be embarrassed. It's no big deal."

Gloria gave her a grin that creeped her out. It reminded her of a clown she had seen in a horror movie once. "Oh, I know it's no big deal. In fact, I'm almost glad it happened, because it brought Chad and me closer together."

What? *What is she talking about?* "I'm glad to hear that," she said because she couldn't think of anything else to say.

Gloria started kicking again. Cold water splashed onto Heidi's legs. She tried to ignore it.

"Oh, I'm so sure you are glad," Gloria cooed. "It was really quite lovely. He came to apologize, and then we went for a long walk in the woods. It was so beautiful, just getting to spend some time with him alone." She gave the word "alone" extra emphasis.

"That's great. Well, enjoy your time here by the water—alone." She tried to give the word as much venom as Gloria had given it. She started to get up, but then paused. "How's your hamstring?"

She stopped kicking. "Fine."

"Did the long walk make the pain worse?"

Gloria didn't answer.

"Are the herbs helping?"

"I wouldn't know. I haven't been taking them."

*Enough.* Heidi was beyond annoyed. She had prepared those herbs herself. It had taken her time and energy.

She took a deep breath and reminded herself that this wasn't about her. Gloria was paying a chunk of change to stay at Serenity Hills, and that money covered those herbs, whether she consumed them or not. Heidi tried to be graceful as she stood up and walked away from the woman with the perfect toes.

Heidi had work to do, but she wasn't in the mood. She found a hammock—not the one Gloria had used; she figured that one might have bad mojo—and lay down.

Why was she so upset about what she had just learned? So what if two guests had gone for a walk together? Chad didn't belong to her. They weren't in a relationship. But still, she was hurt and offended by his bad taste. She told herself she wouldn't be as annoyed if he had gone for a walk with any other woman in the world. But Gloria? Gloria was insufferable.

Heidi had only been in the hammock for five minutes when she gave up and climbed out. It was no use trying to relax. Her brain was a hamster on a wheel. She needed something to distract her. She headed for the library.

Naihma was already there. "Hey, Heidi! Here to do some more research?"

"No, just looking for some pleasure reading."

"I'm afraid to say that I think some of our recent guests have pilfered our collection. It seems all that's left are books about health and romance novels."

Heidi's stomach churned. She'd read all the health books, and she certainly wasn't in the mood for romance. She needed a good thriller, or even better, a post-apocalyptic drama— something good and dreary. "Where did all the other books go? Did we have a yard sale that I missed?"

Naihma chuckled. "As bizarre as it is, the only thing I can think of is that some of our guests walked off with the books. But that's hard to believe, as most of our clients are fairly well-to-do to be stealing old paperbacks."

"They're probably taking them for the flight." Heidi knew that a lot of their clients came from afar.

"That's a good theory! Maybe you missed

your calling as a detective."

Heidi snickered. "Hardly. I don't think I'm a very good judge of character." She picked up a book, but the man's naked chest on the cover was far too shiny for her taste. She put it back and pulled out another. This chest was even shinier. Did they rub those cover models down with oil?

"Well, best wishes for finding something delightful. I'm going to go."

"Wait!"

Naihma turned around and looked at her expectantly.

"I'm having some trouble helping Gloria. I'm embarrassed to admit it. It's never happened to me before. But she seems resistant to my help. She's not taking my herbs, and she won't give me any details about her injury. Do you know any more about it than I do? I read her entry paperwork, but the details were slim. I don't even understand the extent of her injury. And I see no evidence that there's any injury at all!" Her voice rose in fervor as she spoke.

Naihma raised an eyebrow. "Are you suggesting what I think you're suggesting?"

"I'm not suggesting anything." *Oh no. I just got myself in trouble.*

"Good. Because for a second it almost sounded as though you were accusing Gloria of faking an injury. And that would be foolish.

That doesn't even make sense. People don't need to be injured to come here. She wouldn't need to make up any excuse at all. She could have just come."

"You're right." Heidi hadn't thought of that. "I'm sorry."

"It's okay. But even if she is lying, we shouldn't be accusing her of it. I don't want us accusing our clients of anything, ever." She looked at the bookshelf. "Except maybe paperback theft after they've left."

Heidi snickered. "I really didn't mean to accuse her of anything. It's just bizarre. It's like she's keeping the injury a secret and won't let me treat her."

Naihma's expression softened. She took a step toward Heidi. "I understand. But you know by now that some people aren't ready to heal when they get to us. Just do the best you can. I can't ask for anything more than your best." Naihma gave her shoulder an encouraging squeeze and then turned to go.

Heidi realized, not for the first time, that she had the best boss in the world. Her heart swelled with gratitude—for Naihma, for her job, and for Serenity Hills.

When Naihma got to the doorway, she turned back toward Heidi. "By the way, how *are* you and Mr. LaChance getting along?"

Heidi pictured Gloria and him out for their

long walk. Then wondered why that image had flashed through her mind. That had nothing to do with the question Naihma had asked. "We're getting along fine. He's a lot more down to earth than I thought he would be. And he's very open to accepting my help. When he got here, he didn't think we could do anything for him. Now he keeps saying he can't believe how good he feels."

Naihma beamed with pride. "See! Those are the guests who make it all worthwhile."

Yeah, Chad was making her job something all right, but she wasn't sure "worthwhile" was quite the right word.

On Chad's way to the kitchen for his morning yerba maté—he was actually starting to look forward to the murky green elixir—he glimpsed Heidi in the hallway, but she ducked into another hall before he was anywhere near her as if challenging him to a round of hide and seek. He looked down that hallway when he got there, but she was nowhere in sight. Just in case she *wasn't* trying to play a game, he opted not to chase her.

He was halfway through his second cup of caffeine when Gloria found him in the kitchen.

"Let's go for a walk!" No greeting. No preamble. And if she was still upset about the yoga incident, she wasn't letting it show.

Chad didn't know what to say. He stammered, "Uh …"

"Oh, don't be a spoilsport. I won't bite. Come on, let's go. It will be fun." She grabbed hold of his arm with both hands and began to pull him off his stool.

He certainly did not want to go for a walk with this woman. But he wasn't sure how to say no to her, because he didn't want to hurt her feelings two days in a row. Plus, what else did he have to do?

So he gulped the last of his yerba maté, which was still too hot to gulp, and followed her out through the sliding glass door and into the garden. She headed for the forest like a woman on a mission, and he grudgingly followed, remembering when he had recently followed Heidi toward the same woods. He had felt much more confident then. This time he felt a little like the prey of a black widow spider.

Why *had* Heidi been avoiding him? Or had she been? Maybe she truly hadn't seen him. No, she had seen him. She wasn't blind. She had acted like he used to when he saw high school classmates in the grocery store: pretend you're oblivious and sprint to the checkout. These days his housekeeper did all of his shopping, so these awkward encounters didn't happen to him anymore, but he remembered. He smiled, thinking of how surprised Agnes would be when she heard about his new taste buds. He would have to make sure she added pineapples to the regular grocery list. And did he even own a juicer? His kitchen featured every gadget under the sun, but he didn't think he had a juicer. He made a mental note to ask Heidi what kind of juicer he should buy.

"Yoo-hoo!" Gloria called. "Are you coming?" She had reached the head of the trail, where she stopped and waited for him to catch up, which he did, his legs feeling heavier with each step.

They started walking side by side, into the trees.

Suddenly, somehow her hand was in his, her fingers intertwined with his as if they did this all the time, as if it came perfectly naturally to them. He wasn't sure what to do. He wasn't sure he had ever been in such a situation. Maybe in junior high. He tried to remember how he would have handled such a scenario in seventh grade.

"Uh ... Gloria? I don't mean to be unfriendly, but I'm not comfortable holding hands with you."

She dropped his hand in a jiffy and smiled up at him with wide, innocent eyes. "Oh, I'm so sorry. You are absolutely right." She was almost baby-talking. Did she think he was a toddler? "I know you want to go slowly."

*Go slowly with what?*

"Don't worry. I want to take things slowly too. I want to enjoy every minute. Slow and steady wins the race!" She giggled.

His unease morphed into absolute dread. He had to get out of the woods. He had to get away from this kooky dancer. He feared the yoga had stirred up the bats in her belfry. "Um, Gloria? I don't know how I misled you, but I'm not interested in having a relationship with anyone." *At least, not with you.*

She tittered. It sounded like a delirious seagull.

"So, how do you like living in Beacon Hill?" she asked.

He started. Beacon Hill? He actually lived in Jamaica Plain, but he did have a condo in Beacon Hill. But how did she know that? *I guess I should be thankful she doesn't know where my house is.* He remembered then that he *was* a rich bachelor who occasionally made the local tabloids. He shouldn't be too surprised. Or alarmed. "Uh ... I like Beacon Hill."

She giggled as if he'd said something witty. "I would *love* to live in Beacon Hill. What a great place to raise a family! Although I really love living in Lincolntown. I think it's the prettiest neighborhood in Boston. I live at 1091 Entex Street, in a duplex. A brick duplex. I live right beside an upscale bar. There are lots and lots of bars in Lincolntown. It's mostly an Irish neighborhood." She giggled again.

Chad wished he were somewhere else. *Anywhere else.*

"But it's not loud or anything. It's lively! Always something to do. Lots of interesting people to talk to. Lots of artists and art events. Do you like art, Chad?"

He'd been to Lincolntown. The only art there was graffiti. He shrugged. "I don't really have time for art."

She leaned into him and laughed again.
Either she was on some drug or she found him
hysterical. Or both.

"Did you know I'm part Irish? Not many
people know that. Not that it's a secret or
anything. I'm proud of my heritage. But I think
my fabulous tan confuses people. My
neighbors are great. The woman who lives in
the other side of my house has an awesome
dog. He's big and brown and fluffy and
friendly—"

"I don't really like dogs." This wasn't true, but
he was trying to get her to stop talking.

"Oh, me *neither*," she said, as if the very
idea was positively dreadful, even though five
seconds ago she'd been gaga for Scooby.
"Lincolntown is very safe. We have a
neighborhood watch program."

He sincerely doubted this.

"Our schools are fantastic. We've gotten lots
of awards for being exemplary. I can't wait to
have lots of children to send to school. Do you
want children, Chad?"

He definitely did, someday. "No. Sure don't."

"Not that I wouldn't mind raising our children
in Beacon Hill. That would be even better.
Although"—she giggled again—"Lincolntown's
parks are so beautiful. So many birds ..."

*Our children?!* This woman was insane.

He'd *been* to Lincolntown. There were no parks. There was only asphalt and crime. He didn't even think birds flew through there. Did she think he was stupid? He started to walk faster and tried to think about something else, tried to enjoy the sunshine and the smells around him, but the scent of flowers reminded him of Heidi. He wondered what she was doing right now. *Had* she been avoiding him this morning—

Gloria elbowed him in the side. Hard enough to hurt. Her elbows were exceptionally picked. "Well?"

He stepped away from her weaponized funny bone. "Uh ... sorry. What were you saying?"

"I invited you to come *visit*! But you're just staring off into space. That's so rude!"

He took another step away. "Sorry, and *no*, I don't think I'll be able to visit. I've got a lot to do when I get home. I don't do much socializing. No time."

She sidled up to him, closing the gap he'd worked so hard to create, and took his hand again. Her hand was like a vise. She leaned into him suggestively and looked up at him with wide eyes. "You know what they say?" She grinned maniacally, and he honestly feared for his safety.

"No, what?"

"All work and no play makes Chad a dull boy." She snorted, and he tried to jerk away, but she held him fast.

The path they'd been walking on spilled out into a clearing, and he looked up to see that they'd made a big loop and returned to the garden, where he saw something he really didn't want to see in that moment: Heidi.

She looked up at them, and then looked down at the weeds she was pulling. He waited for her to look up again, to acknowledge their presence, but she didn't.

"If you'll excuse me," he said to Gloria, forcefully extracting his hand from her clutch, "I'm not feeling well, and I've got to talk to my health coach." He practically ran to where Heidi was kneeling in the dirt, and squatted beside her. "I thought Meetika was the gardener."

Heidi grabbed a fistful of green and chucked it behind her. She seemed to be using excessive vigor for the task. Was she in a weeding contest? She chucked another handful, and he wondered what plants she was weeding. She didn't seem to be leaving any behind. She did not look up at him or answer him. Just kept pulling and chucking.

He was overwhelmed with guilt. But this led to anger. What did he have to feel guilty about? He hadn't done anything wrong. So he stood and walked away.

## 20

Heidi listened to his footsteps fade away. She hadn't looked up at him because she was working very hard not to cry, and she thought that if she looked into those brown eyes of his, her tears would fall.

The fact that she was near tears at all made her furious with herself. What was it about this guy that had her brain acting like it had vacated the building? He was nothing special. Just some rich, pompous snob from the big city. So why did the sight of Gloria and him hand-in-hand make her sick to her stomach?

She had to get a grip. She had to stop acting like a ninny. She looked down at what, only moments before, had been a bountiful patch of cinnamon basil. It was now a barren patch of dirt. She was going to have to get some more basil plants somewhere. Chad was right. Meetika was the gardener, and she wouldn't be pleased with what Heidi had done there. Also, Bob used basil for many of his culinary exploits. He would certainly notice someone had slaughtered all of his favorite herb.

She sat back on her heels and let out a long breath. She wiped at her eyes with the backs of her hands, leaving dirt streaks on her cheeks. She had to be professional. That was the answer. No matter what happened in the next few days, she would be one hundred percent professional with Chad. She would be his health coach. She would help him get healthy. And then she would watch him sail off into the sunset. That was the way it was supposed to be. He was never supposed to be more than a client. She didn't know how she had gotten so caught up in other silly ideas and feelings. She stood up slowly, feeling better now that she had a plan.

She found him behind the main building in the horseshoe pit all by himself. "One thing about playing all alone," she called out. "You'll always win." As soon as the words left her mouth, her cheeks got hot. Why had she said that? What a ridiculous thing to say.

*Professional. Be professional.*

"Or you'll always lose. It depends on your perspective." He stared at her expectantly, his posture stiff.

She walked down the sloping lawn to reach his spot in the shade. "Well, the fresh air will do you good either way. How are you feeling? Any more detox symptoms?"

"You seem to be in better spirits," he said.

There was no use pretending that their last encounter hadn't happened. "I'm sorry, Chad. I was unprofessional the last time we spoke. I had a lot on my mind, and I took it out on you. Please forgive me."

Half his mouth curled upward. "Are you sure that's it?"

She took a step closer, but then she decided that was dangerous, and she stepped back. "Yes, I'm sure."

"I got the impression you might have been mad at me." He paused as if waiting for her to say something. Then he added, his voice lower than usual, "I thought maybe you were upset about Gloria and me, about what you saw—"

"Oh no!" Heidi said with too much enthusiasm. "I love seeing our guests getting along. It's so good for people to bond with each other. Naihma says it makes people come back here more often if they make friends here." *Great. Now I'm babbling.*

"I see." He didn't look convinced. He took two steps toward her.

Her brain told her to take another step back, but the rest of her body refused to move.

"Well, I wanted you to know that there's absolutely nothing going on between Gloria and me."

Why was he lying? Maybe he wasn't the nice guy she thought he was. Clearly, there was *something* going on. Gloria had told her as much, and minutes ago, she'd witnessed them coming out of the woods all snuggled up together.

"She grabbed my hand against my will, and I was trying not to be cruel to her. I didn't want another incident like at the yoga shack."

Part of her was certain he was lying. Part of her was desperate to believe him. "It's the yoga *hut*. It's not a *shack*." Why was she getting so defensive about the yoga hut? She was really losing her mind.

"I'm sorry." He took another step closer.

What was he doing?

"I didn't mean to insult the yoga hut." He spoke the last word with affection. "Wanna play horseshoes?"

She did want to play horseshoes, because she wanted to be close to him. But she didn't want to spend any more time with him, because she didn't want to grow any more attached.

He raised an eyebrow. "That wasn't supposed to be a trick question. Are you trying to keep me in suspense?"

What if he told Naihma that she had refused to help him get exercise? "Sure, I'd love to play horseshoes with you."

"Great." He grinned, and it took her breath away. "Because I really don't know how."

She returned his smile, and, giving him a wide berth, led him back to the pit. She picked up two horseshoes. "I'll go first." She dragged her toe through the dirt to make a line. "There.

You can't cross that line."

He saluted her. "Yes, ma'am."

She tried not to smile but failed. He was so cute. "And then you just throw." She bent over and tossed the horseshoe toward the stake. It made a clanking sound and bounced off.

"What does that mean?"

"It means I didn't get any points. You've probably heard the saying, 'Close only counts in grenades and horseshoes?' Well, it has to be within a horseshoe's width to get any points."

"Okay." He bumped her hip with his. "My turn." He bent, his brow furrowed in concentration.

She suppressed a giggle.

He let go, and the edge of the shoe caught the stake and spun around it, landing at the bottom of the stake. "Woo-hoo!" he cried, and then he held up a hand for a high five, which she reluctantly granted. "It's touching the stake! So I get a point, right?"

"It's actually a ringer, because it's surrounding the stake. And it's worth *three* points ... Unless!" she said dramatically.

"Unless what?"

"*Unless* I cover *your* ringer with *my* ringer." She raised both eyebrows.

"I'd like to see you try."

She bumped his hip out of the way, just as

he had done to her. *You're not being very professional right now, Heidi.* Oh well. She threw her second horseshoe, and it missed by a mile.

"Choke!" he coughed into his hand.

She looked at him. "Not funny."

He stepped up to the line. "What happens if I throw two ringers?"

"Don't worry. You won't."

"Challenge!" he cried. He threw the shoe, and it went nowhere near the stake.

She giggled. "All right. Three to one. But enjoy your lead, because it's not going to last."

He gently jabbed her with his elbow. "Cocky, aren't we?"

She led him to the other end of the pit and picked up her shoes. Then she drew another line in the dirt. "Here we go."

"Why do you always get to go first?"

She stepped back. "Fine, ya big baby. Go ahead."

He gave her a triumphant smile and stepped up. He threw. It came close, but no cigar. She threw. It came closer than his. She smiled at him. "I'm nipping at your heels."

He threw again. No luck.

She threw again, held her breath as the metal shoe flew through the air, and then squealed when it landed within an inch of the stake. "Two to three, baby! I hope you enjoy your lead while you have it!"

Thirty minutes later, the score was 38 to 34. Heidi had gone ahead, but she wasn't confident she would stay in the lead. It was suspicious how good he was at a game he'd never played before.

She couldn't imagine how she had gotten so into the game. She usually had no competitive spirit, but for some reason, she *couldn't* let Chad beat her at this game.

It was her turn. She launched her shoe, and it came within a few inches of the stake. She cheered.

"You sure do have good form," Chad said, stepping up to the line.

"Don't you be looking at my form!"

He laughed and let go of the horseshoe. It flew through the air, end over end, and then fell perfectly in place around the stake. He jumped up and down, cheering.

She stared at him, amused, until he calmed down.

"What?" he asked.

She shook her head. "Nothing. I was just thinking, you *really* seem to be enjoying this. Do you get to play games very often?"

He shrugged. "I have a racquetball court."

"But do you use it?"

He scrunched up his face. "Not really."

She shook her head. "All right. Get out of my

way." She stepped up to the line. If she could cover his ringer, she'd win the game. She threw. For a moment, it looked as though she had done it, but then the shoe landed with a soft thud in the sand, just shy of the stake.

"Here we go!" He stepped up. "All I need is another ringer!"

She snorted. "Yeah, right."

He quirked an eyebrow. "You doubt me?"

"I doubt you," she said without looking at him. She was staring at the stake, her belly twisted with nerves.

He exaggerated his windup, making her laugh, and then he let go. It almost felt like slow motion: she watched the shoe soar through the air and then she watched it land, completely encircling the stake.

But then life sped up to a breakneck pace as Chad picked her up off the ground and spun her around in the air. It took her breath away, and she grabbed his shoulders to try to steady herself.

"Victory is mine!" he cried, laughing. Then he set her down, his hands still on her waist, and time stood still.

She knew she should pull away, but she couldn't make herself do it. He was staring into her eyes as if asking permission. She didn't give it, but she didn't deny it either. And then his lips were on hers, softly at first. Her knees went weak, but he held her up. Her lips parted on their own, without her consent, and Chad pulled her body into his. Fire shot through her body. She had been kissed before, but never like this. Every cell in her body felt that kiss.

So much for being professional. Abruptly, she pulled away, putting her hand over her mouth. "I'm sorry, Chad. That shouldn't have happened. I shouldn't have let that happen." She turned and ran up the sloping lawn and into the house.

She shut the door behind her and then leaned on it, trying to catch her breath. *How dare he?* Who did he think he was? Walk around holding hands with Gloria and then kiss her like that an hour later. What a player!

## 21

Chad stayed at the horseshoe pit, flinging shoes at the stake. Should he have kissed her? Yes, definitely. No matter what happened, that kiss had been worth it. Unless of course, she hadn't *wanted* him to kiss her. But she had. Her lips had made that clear. So why had she run away?

He flung another horseshoe, this one with too much oomph. Suddenly, he was overwhelmed with a desire to just go home. He felt healthier. He knew he must *be* healthier, with all the fruits and herbs he'd been consuming. But his mentor had said he had to spend the *whole week* at Serenity Hills. If he went home early, would it void his deal? Part of him didn't care.

He took a deep breath. *This is what happens with idle hands. You end up with a crush on your health coach.* He turned away from the horseshoe pit and headed back toward the main building.

Heidi obviously wasn't into him. Or was she? It wasn't just the kiss that made him think so. There had been other moments when she had seemed to be attracted to him, or at least interested in him. But then other times she was cool as a cucumber. Maybe she was just the moodiest woman in the world. Either way, maybe he should avoid her for the next three days. He didn't need some complicated drama to extract himself from when it was time to go home.

He decided he would focus on getting some rest. Even if the boredom killed him. He would hide in his room. The idea of holding still for so long with no way to plug in to the real world made him feel ill. Why didn't they have Wi-Fi? Or cell service? Were they trying to kill him?

*I know!* He had a brilliant idea. They had a library. Maybe they had some entrepreneurial books or some self-development books. He could exercise his business brain that way. Saul would be thrilled. He'd already read the classics, like *7 Habits of Highly Effective People* and *Miracle Morning*. But rereading these formative books wouldn't hurt him. He fervently hoped they had such books.

They didn't. They had books about how to clean out your gallbladder, how to have healthy skin, how to alkalize the body, and how to heal leaky gut. They had at least fifty books on weight loss, and that many again on herbal healing. There was also a book on chicken health, which was odd, he thought, for a place with no chickens. Then they had two shelves chock-full of well-worn romance novels. He closed his eyes for a second, and then scanned the shelves again, certain that these could not be his only choices.

"Slim pickings, I'm afraid," a voice said from behind him.

He turned to see Fawsa, the village counselor. "No kidding."

"How are you?"

"I'm fine. Just bored."

Fawsa didn't look convinced. "Want to go find a comfy spot and chat?"

He really didn't want to do this. "No thanks. Not much of a chatter."

"I'd be happy to write a letter to your executive coach, tell him how confident I am that you'll be making healthier choices from now on."

Chad furrowed his brow.

"I read your file. I know he twisted your arm to get you here."

Chad let out a long breath. "You'd really write a letter?" Maybe he *could* go home early.

Fawsa flashed him a broad smile. "If you come with me to find a comfy spot and chat!"

He sighed. She was bribing him. So not cool. But, what else did he have to do? He shrugged. "Okay."

"Great. Inside or outside?"

He wondered where Gloria was and decided she was probably outside. "Inside."

"Great! Follow me."

He followed her down the hallway toward

the lounge.

"Will this do?" she asked.

He looked around. Not much privacy. "Don't you have an office?"

"I do, but I'm afraid it's not very comfortable. If you want to discuss confidential stuff, we can certainly go there, though."

He didn't want to discuss confidential stuff. He didn't want to discuss anything. "No, this will be fine." He let himself sink into one of the plush armchairs. She took the couch.

*Well, this is backward.*

"So, Chad, tell me about yourself."

Chad squirmed in his chair. He really hated this stuff. "Not much to tell, I guess. I grew up in Western Massachusetts in a healthy, happy family. No trauma there to process or to blame for all my problems."

She raised an eyebrow. "What problems do you mean?"

Uh-oh. By trying to be a smart aleck, he'd stepped right into it. "I didn't mean anything. I don't have any problems."

"Everyone has problems, Chad." She tilted her head to the side and gave him a small smile.

Ugh. What had he done? He wanted to get out of there. "No really, I don't. I've got my dream career. I've got more money than I need. I really don't have any complaints."

Her head was still tilted. "We both know that's not true."

Obviously, she was going to sit there and smile at him until he shared a problem with her. He scanned his brain for a problem, any problem. "Well, at the moment, I think I have a stalker."

Fawsa's eyes lit up. This woman really loved her job. "A stalker? Tell me more."

He shrugged. "It's no big deal really. It's ..." He lowered his voice. "The dancer, Gloria? She thinks we're in a relationship, and I have done *nothing* to encourage that. But she's planning our future, talking about having children ... I think I'm going to have to hire extra bodyguards when I get—"

"Well, I never!" A red-faced Gloria materialized in the lounge's entryway. "How *dare* you speak about me like that! This is slander! I'll have you in court! Maybe then you'll know what a *real problem* is!" Without allowing any time for retort, she turned and glided down the hallway. Even when she was mad as a hornet, she was still graceful.

He turned back toward Fawsa. "Maybe we should have met in your office."

Fawsa's face flushed red. "I am so, so sorry. Nothing like that has happened here before. I meet with guests in here all the time. I didn't even think anyone could hear us from the hallway."

Chad held up a hand to stop her apology. "It's okay, really. I don't care. I told you. She's"—he pointed a finger at his temple and twirled it. "Just know that, if you find me poisoned in my sleep, it was her."

Fawsa's eyes grew wide. "Does your door lock?"

He laughed. "No, no, I was only kidding. I don't think she'll try to hurt me. Well, it's been fun, but I think I'm going to go find a book." He started to stand.

"Wait!" Fawsa held up a hand so authoritatively that he sat back down. "We're not done. I need to ask you a serious question."

*Uh-oh.* "What?"

"Who do you have in your life?"

He didn't understand the question. "You mean romantically?"

"No, I mean like *anyone*. Any human being you have a relationship with."

"Well, I have my mentor, and my CFO, and my assistant—"

"No. Those are people who do things for you. You pay them to be in a relationship with you. Do you have anybody you don't pay? What about your nonprofit work? Are you close to any of your volunteers? Maybe at your youth rec center?"

He blinked, surprised. Then he remembered that people here thought he was some sort of mega-philanthropist. "Oh ... uh ... no. I don't know any of them personally."

"So you have no one?"

His chest grew tight. "I have my family."

"Don't get defensive, Chad. I'm not criticizing you. I'm only trying to help. It's not healthy to go through life without companionship. How often do you see your family?"

*Almost never.* He looked down at his lap and started to pick pieces of fuzz off his shorts. "Not very often."

Fawsa leaned forward in her chair. "I *know* you are hyper-successful, and I wouldn't want to change that for the world. I'm just wondering how much *more* successful you'd be if you didn't try to do it all alone."

## 22

Heidi was ravenous. She'd gone for a long jog through the woods to try to clear her head. It had worked. Then she'd taken a long bath. Now she was ready to eat a salad the size of a truck, even though it was past her bedtime. She was surprised to find Bob in the kitchen.

"What are you still doing in here?" she asked.

"The same thing you are, I presume. I came to get a snack. Have a seat. I'll whip you up something."

"You don't have to do that. I can fend for myself."

"I know that, but I want to. Besides"—he leaned in closer—"I have some exceptionally juicy gossip to share."

She fervently hoped it wasn't about Chad and Gloria. Or Chad *or* Gloria. "Oh yeah? What?"

He pulled a bowl of kale out of the fridge. "First, I heard Chad talking to Fawsa in the lounge."

Heidi groaned. "Bob! I've told you a hundred times to stop eavesdropping on Fawsa's sessions!"

"And I've told her a hundred times to stop holding them in the lounge. What psychologist does that?"

Heidi shrugged. Fawsa did lots of things she didn't understand. "Whatever you heard, I don't want to know. It's none of my business."

Bob completely ignored her. "Chad said he was afraid of Gloria—that she was his *stalker.*"

Heidi felt her eyes grow wide and tried to stop them. "What? That's insane."

"Yeah. He sounded pretty freaked out, but wait—it gets better." Bob leaned on the counter and lowered his voice even more. He looked *so* thrilled to be serving this gossip up that Heidi had to giggle at him. "A few minutes ago, I caught Gloria in the office."

"*Our* office?" Heidi asked and then felt silly. What other office could he be talking about?

Bob nodded. "Yep. Our office. Where she's not supposed to be. Using the phone she's not supposed to use without permission."

This time Heidi allowed her eyes to grow wide. "Do you know who she called?"

"I don't, but you won't believe what she said." He stood up and shoved a giant leaf of kale into his mouth. He was going to make her beg.

"Tell me!" she screeched.

"She told whoever it was that she was here 'with Chad.'" He made air quotes around the last two words, which was funny, because he was still holding a bunch of kale in one hand.

Heidi did *not* like the sound of that. "What?"

Bob nodded. "Yep. She said they'd come here together. And she said that they'd had a big fight, and that she was breaking up with him and coming home."

Heidi laughed so suddenly she snorted. Her hand flew to cover her mouth and nose, but then she moved it to say, "What else?"

"She said, and I quote, 'I'm so frustrated. I've been out of work for six weeks, and he doesn't even *care*. He could pull some strings to get me some more jobs, but he *won't*.'" He delivered the quotation in a falsetto that made Heidi laugh until her sides hurt.

"That doesn't even make sense," she said when she'd recovered. "How could *Chad* get her dancing jobs? I mean, I know he's rich and all, but that doesn't mean he can pull strings in the dance world, does it?"

Bob shrugged. "I'm not sure Gloria thinks like we do. You know—*rationally*."

"Is there more?" Heidi asked. She really wanted there to be more.

"You're not putting two and two together."

"What?" What was she missing?

He leaned on the counter again. "If she's been out of work for *six weeks*, then she obviously didn't hurt her leg in a *performance*."

Heidi gasped. "Oh! You're *right*."

"Yeah, and I'm betting she didn't even hurt her leg at all. I'm thinking she *only* came here because Chad was here. Maybe she really *is* his stalker." He stood up and took another bite of kale. "I don't know if she wants to marry him and steal all his money, or if she just wants him to buy her a job, but either way, the woman is shady."

Heidi shrugged. "Or maybe she's in love with him."

Bob gave her a knowing look she didn't appreciate. "She's not acting like she loves him. She's acting like she's trying to manipulate him. I feel bad for the guy."

"Yeah." Heidi nodded. "I do too—now." Maybe she'd been wrong about him—about *them*. He *had* told her that Gloria forced him to take a walk with her. Maybe she really had. Maybe there was nothing going on. And maybe he wasn't a player.

But it didn't matter to her. Or at least, it *shouldn't*. Because she shouldn't be having feelings for the billionaire. She shouldn't be having crazy ideas. They were from two different worlds, and even if he would consider being with her, she liked the world she was in.

## 23

Chad lay on his back in the cool soil of the garden, looking up at the stars. Heidi lay beside him, on her side, her head propped up on her elbow so she was looking down at him.

He smiled at her. Something tickled his ankle. *Stupid ticks.* He shook his leg, and the tickling stopped. He smiled at Heidi again, a big goofy smile.

She smiled back, and Chad wondered if she was going to kiss him. He wanted her to.

This time the tick tickled the bottom of his foot, and he used his other foot to knock it off his skin. It occurred to him that he should be worried about such a persistent arachnid, but he was too busy gazing into Heidi's mesmerizing eyes.

He rolled over to face her, and propped his head up with his arm. They came face to face. He leaned in for the kiss he knew was coming, and a fierce pinch drew his attention to his big toe.

He looked down to see that Gloria was sitting at his feet glowering at him, with her hand perched just above the injured toe. "Ow!" he cried, feeling more violated than injured.

He sat up abruptly and looked around in the darkness. After a few panic-stricken seconds, he fell back into bed.

It was just a dream. Thank God. It had all seemed so real. *Does detox cause crazy nightmares?*

He pulled the covers up to his chin and tried to calm his heart rate. He did some deep breathing, like Heidi had taught him, and he slowly relaxed.

But he couldn't fall back asleep. The minutes ticked by. He tossed and turned, tried every position, and flipped his pillow numerous times. But it wasn't a lack of comfort that was keeping him awake. It was Heidi.

He couldn't stop thinking about her. Sure, she had been moody lately, even before he kissed her, but he remembered well the Heidi of his first two days at Serenity Hills. She had been so joyful. What was wrong with her now? He missed the Heidi he'd first met.

He propped himself up onto some extra pillows so that he could look out at the moon-drenched property. It really was beautiful here. The scene brought him an unexpected sense of peace. As he stared at the moon, he saw motion out of the corner of his eye.

There was Heidi, slowly walking across the lawn in a short nightie. He caught himself looking at her legs and willed himself to stop. She didn't know she was being watched, obviously, so he shouldn't be checking out her legs. He watched her walk across the lawn, her steps light. Then she climbed into a hammock, folded her arms so that her head lay in her hands, and looked up at the moon. He was oddly touched by the fact that they had both decided to moon watch at the same time, and he even entertained the idea of going outside to watch it with her. He talked himself out of it though—didn't want to make her run away again—and then fell asleep while watching her watch the sky.

A light tapping on his door woke him. He looked out his window; Heidi was no longer in the hammock. He didn't know how long he'd slept, but as he groped around for his phone to tell him what time it was, the rapping on the door intensified, so he gave up on his time check and climbed out of bed.

He unlocked and opened the door to find Gloria, scantily clad, standing in front of him. She didn't even say anything. She just flung her arms around his neck and started kissing him. The force of the impact made him stagger backward into his room. It took him only seconds to peel her off, but the seconds felt exceptionally long.

"Gloria!" he said, his tone firm. "Enough! We are not in a relationship. We will never be in a relationship. I am tired of this game. I am telling you now, officially, that I do not want to have any social contact with you—*ever*. If you continue harassing me, I will be forced to take legal action. And believe me, you *do not* want to meet my lawyers." He knew he was being harsh. He also knew he'd been pushed past his limit.

Gloria burst into tears and put her hands over her face. She babbled something, but he couldn't make out what she was saying. He also didn't care. She had gone too far. He actually felt violated.

"Gloria, leave my room. Now."

"You don't understand!"

"You're right. I most certainly do not understand. But I don't need to understand. None of this is my problem. You need to understand that you need to leave my room right now. Or I will go get Naihma."

She lifted her head and looked at him. "But I *love* you!"

He took a deep breath. "No, Gloria. You don't love me. And you need to get some help. Do you want me to go get Fawsa?"

Her eyes narrowed. "Don't you dare," she said sibilantly.

He took a step back.

Slowly, she turned to go. She paused with her back turned to him as if deciding what to do next. Then she left his room, and he shut the door behind her. He turned the lock, grateful for the first time for his conversation with Fawsa. If she hadn't asked him about whether or not his door had a lock, he might never have thought to lock it. He turned the knob and pulled, just to make sure the lock held. Then he went back to bed, though he was certain he was done sleeping for the night.

He fluffed his pillows, pulled the covers to his chin, and looked at the moon.

## 24

Heidi lay in the hammock, staring up at the heavens. The beauty of it, the majesty, took her breath away. She hadn't been doing this enough lately. Maybe it was a good thing she hadn't been able to fall asleep.

She was tired because she hadn't been sleeping well the previous few nights, but she couldn't quite make herself fall asleep, even as relaxed as she was out here under the stars. Every time she came close to drifting off, her brain would drift to Chad. What it had been like to feel his lips on hers. How it had felt to have his arms tight around her. What would it be like to be a billionaire's girlfriend? To be able to travel wherever she wanted, be a guest at health retreats like the one she worked at, and have ample resources to help others in need? Then she would jerk herself out of her reverie. There was no use daydreaming about such things. It could never work. They were too different.

Suddenly, she felt someone watching her. She looked around the well-lit yard. The moonlight was almost as bright as dawn. She didn't see anything and lay back down. It occurred to her that in her current setting, if there *was* something watching her, it would be completely benign. There was nothing dangerous in Serenity Hills. Except for maybe Gloria. Heidi snickered. And Gloria probably wasn't a danger to Heidi—only Chad.

She tried to count the stars, but by the time she got to eighty, she was still wide awake and the counting was driving her nuts. Disappointed that the hammock wasn't going to induce sleep any better than her bed had, she dismounted and slowly made her way inside, her warm feet tickled by the cool grass.

She opened the door slowly so as not to make any creaking sound, even though no one slept anywhere near the main entrance. Then she tiptoed down the hallways that led to staff quarters and her room. She didn't turn on any lights because she didn't want to bother anyone. It was much darker inside than it had been under the moon, so she felt along the wall with one hand. She had navigated this building many times in the dark and was quite comfortable doing so. This was her home, and she knew every inch of it.

She had just rounded a sharp corner when she smashed into someone.

"Ow! Watch where you're going! What's wrong with you?"

Heidi recognized the voice. She squinted in the darkness, trying to read Gloria's expression. Was she really in physical pain? She couldn't tell. "I'm so sorry! I wasn't expecting to meet anyone."

"Well, why are you sneaking around in the dark?" Gloria hissed.

"I'm not sneaking anywhere. I'm just going to my room. What are you doing here? This isn't anywhere near your—"

An ugly realization dawned on her then. This hallway did not lead to Gloria's room, or anywhere near it. But it did lead to Chad's.

"Oh," Gloria said with a new seductive edge to her voice, "I have a perfectly good reason for being here. I was just leaving Chad's room. He said I had better go, or he wouldn't get any sleep at all." She leaned closer to Heidi, gave her a sinister wink, and then purposely bumped into her shoulder as she walked past her and continued down the hallway.

Suddenly Heidi was very hot. A lump formed in her throat. She was so confused. If Gloria was lying, she was very good at it. Maybe she wasn't a stalker after all. Or maybe she was a stalker, and Chad didn't mind being stalked. Either way, it was another red flag to discourage her from daydreaming about anything with Chad. Fighting back the tears, she hurried the rest of the way to her room, not caring how much noise she made. Then she shut the door, fell into her bed, and cried herself to sleep.

## 25

On Thursday morning, Chad woke up in an amazingly good mood. Despite the fright he had endured the night before, his new nutrition regimen had his systems firing at a whole new level. Saul had been right to send him to hippie camp. He was going to take a lot of his new habits home with him, not counting the yoga or the traditional sauna of course.

He noticed Heidi sitting on the porch swing by the garden, and he cheerily carried his yerba maté outside. As he slid the glass door shut behind him, she turned to look. He wasn't certain, but he thought he saw contempt in her eyes. *Moody for sure.* She turned back around without saying anything.

He sat down beside her. "Good morning, health coach." There was that lilac scent again. He resisted the urge to lean in closer and sniff her.

"Good morning," she said without looking at him.

"It's a beautiful day out." He cringed at his lack of originality. He wasn't well versed in making small talk, let alone in starting it.

"It certainly is."

"Are you okay?"

"I'm fine."

He wasn't sure what to say, but he didn't

want to just walk away. She was obviously upset. "It's none of my business, but I like you, Heidi. And I'm concerned about you. You're always worried about other people's health, but it seems like some days, you don't feel so good yourself."

Her head snapped up, and she looked at him. "I'm fine. I promise."

"It just seems like sometimes you love it here, but then sometimes you're really sad." He was trying not to use the word "moody," though that would have made it easier to make his point.

She took a deep breath and let it out slowly. Then she took a sip of her beverage. She didn't say anything.

"What made you choose to become a health coach? Seems like a tough gig, having to care about so many other people. And I can't imagine it pays much." He flinched. He should've left off that last part. He hadn't meant it to be rude, but it had certainly come out that way.

"Money means nothing to me."

"I'm sorry. I didn't mean to offend. I am genuinely curious about what made you choose such a selfless career path."

She took another sip. This time it looked as if she was thinking about saying something.

He willed himself to be patient.

Finally, she spoke. "When I was in high school, I wanted to be a forensic scientist. Isn't that ridiculous?" Her mouth smiled, but her eyes didn't. They had a faraway look in them. "I watched too much NCIS, obviously. Abby is like my favorite person in the whole world."

*A fictional character is her favorite person in the whole world? She needs better friends.* "I've never seen it."

She looked at him, her eyes wide. "You're kidding."

He shook his head. "I would never kid about crime drama."

Her eyes stayed big. "It's like the most watched show on television."

"I don't watch much television."

She finally looked away, her shocked expression fading—a little. "Well, that's actually a really healthy habit you have there. But you should watch at least a few episodes, just so you can meet Abby."

"Okay. I will. So, what made you go from forensics to herbs?"

She took a deep breath. "My dad got sick my senior year in high school. Really sick. He didn't have health insurance, and the treatments available to him were very expensive. We all scrambled to raise money. We sold everything we had. I quit playing sports and got a job. Everyone we knew gave him money. People we didn't know gave him money. But it was never enough. I got so angry. It was just so unfair." She paused for so long, he wondered if she would continue. Then she did. "I started out just wanting to help people who couldn't afford to go to the doctor. But the more I learned, the more I knew I could help everyone." She stopped again.

"I'm sorry about your dad. I can relate."

She looked up quickly. "You can?"

He chewed on his lower lip. "I'm afraid so. My dad had a great job, made great money, and had great health insurance. But when he got sick, the best doctors in the world couldn't save him." He looked at her. "I'm not saying that you're wrong. Life *isn't* fair sometimes. *Most* of the time maybe. But sometimes people just leave us, and it's not anyone's fault."

She studied the ground at her feet. "I'm sorry about your dad. How old were you?"

"Nineteen."

She sucked in some air. "Wow, we were both so young."

"Yep. I didn't realize it then, but I was just a kid. I wanted to be a rock star, not an agricultural entrepreneur."

She giggled. "No way."

"Way. I play a mean electric guitar."

Her eyes grew big again, but there was a

dancing light in them this time. He felt as though he was getting lost in those eyes, and forced himself to look away.

"You need to play for us! In the lounge!"

He guffawed. "No thanks. I haven't played in years." He realized what he'd said earlier. "Maybe I shouldn't have said I *play* a mean electric guitar. I should have said *played*. And really, who knows? I might've really stunk. But I was a teenager, and I thought I was awesome."

She giggled again. "You *are* awesome. But that's quite a leap, from garage band to suit and tie."

"Not as big a leap as gothic forensic scientist in pigtails to health coach."

This time she really laughed, and the sound of it made his heart leap. She'd been so sad a moment ago, and he'd managed to turn it around. He was quite pleased with himself.

"So you *do* know Abby!"

"I said I hadn't seen the show. I never said I didn't know who Abby was. *Everyone* knows Abby."

"True. And I'll have you know—I *do* rock the pigtails on occasion."

He had no doubt. He also wanted to see that.

She took a deep breath. "I didn't set out to be a health coach necessarily. That was just the job title they gave me here. I just wanted to learn how to help people help themselves." She finally looked at him. "And that's what I try to do, every day. I love my job. It is true that I don't make a lot of money, but all of my needs are met, and I'm very happy."

"Then why do you seem so unhappy sometimes?" He knew he was pushing, but he was genuinely concerned. His level of concern surprised him, actually.

She broke his gaze and looked out toward the woods. "Sorry. It doesn't happen often. There just seems to be a lot of things going on around me right now that irritate me." She paused. "I shouldn't let them bother me, but I'm still learning how to be a good human in this world."

He smiled at her turn of phrase. "You can help people be healthy from anywhere. Would you ever consider leaving Serenity Hills?"

She looked at him again, and her eyes seemed exceptionally beautiful today. Bright green, like new blades of grass. "I don't want to leave Serenity Hills. This is my home." The words were positive, but her tone sounded sad.

"There's a whole world out there, Heidi."

"I know, but my world is here."

## 26

Heidi greeted Avinash Vemulakonda at the door, welcomed him profusely, and showed him into the lounge. Bob was already there. Heidi gave him a big smile and asked, "Would you go round everybody up?"

Bob scowled. "Since when was that my duty?"

"Please?" There was a hint of pleading in her voice, and Bob's expression softened. She thought he probably knew why she was hesitant to go be social. She didn't want to have to talk to Chad. Or Gloria. Bob disappeared down the hall.

Heidi asked Avinash if he needed any help setting up, and when he declined, she settled into one of the armchairs.

Apparently, Chad was the first one Bob found. He entered the lounge with wide eyes and made a beeline for her. "What's going on?"

"We try to have a guest speaker every Thursday night."

Chad looked at the man up front and then looked at her. "What kind of guest speaker is he?" He sounded incredulous.

Heidi suppressed a giggle. "He's a yogi, a motivational speaker, and a poet. We have him visit every few months."

Chad looked anything but sold. "So he's a contortionist, a con artist, and a poet? That's quite a combination."

"A con artist? That's a little harsh. You don't believe in the power of positive thought?"

"Oh, I believe in the power of positive thought all right. But you can't teach motivation and hard work in a seminar. So somehow these people have had a little success, and then they go around telling others to just do what they did. But you don't get rich by doing what other people did. You get rich by doing what someone hasn't done yet."

"I really don't want to argue the philosophy of wealth with you—"

Chad looked up as though he'd heard something in the hallway. "Quick! Slide over!"

"What?" She was sitting in an armchair. There was nowhere to slide.

His eyes were wide. He looked panic-stricken. "I'm serious. Slide over."

He turned and began to sit beside her, so she slid as far as she could to the left to avoid being squashed. He forced his perfect bottom into the small space. Sure enough, there was room, but barely. His body was pressed up against hers, and they were wedged in there so tightly, she wasn't sure how they would get out.

"Thank you. You have no idea how you just saved me. Now, try to act naturally."

She couldn't help it. She laughed loudly. The yogi looked up, alarmed. "Sorry," she said to him. Then she looked at Chad. "What is wrong with you?"

"I don't want Gloria to sit beside me. It's a long story."

The smile fled her face. So he had spent the night with Gloria and now wanted nothing to do with her. What a jerk! "You're a jerk," she said before she could stop herself.

His head whipped around to look at her. "I am not a jerk, I assure you. You have no idea what she's been putting me through."

"Oh, I have a pretty good idea. She let me have an earful in the hallway outside your room in the middle of the night." Heidi's face grew hotter as she spoke.

Chad didn't say anything at first, and Heidi looked at him to try to read his facial expression. He was looking right at her, and he looked horrified.

"Heidi, I promise you. Nothing happened between Gloria and me. Ever. And it won't happen, ever. I have threatened to take legal action. She did come to my room last night, and she tried to kiss me, and I promptly refused, and told her in no uncertain terms to leave."

Heidi didn't know what to think or say. "But you guys go for long walks in the woods!"

"*One* long walk," he corrected her, "and it was the worst hour of my life."

She giggled and clamped a hand over her mouth. He looked so serious. She shouldn't be laughing at his trauma. If there even *was* any trauma. "Why would she lie to me?"

"I don't know why she does anything. You can believe her if you want, but I wish you wouldn't. I'm a lot of things, but I am not a liar."

Gloria walked into the room then, and Heidi couldn't help herself. She started to giggle. The whole thing was so absurd. Somehow, she knew Chad was telling the truth. Bob had heard Gloria being shady in the office, and it didn't make sense that Chad would welcome a bona fide stalker into his bedroom.

Chad started laughing too, and put a hand over his mouth as if to hold it in, but there was no stemming that tide. His laughter made Heidi laugh even harder. The yogi looked at them suspiciously, and Gloria wheeled around to glare at them. "Can I help you?"

This response was so bizarre that it sent Heidi into another bout of laughter—this one even stronger. She bent forward and put her face in her hands, and concentrated on regaining control of herself.

Naihma and Fawsa walked in then, and their

presence went a long way toward sobering her. Chad continued silently laughing beside her, his whole body shaking, but Heidi maintained her hard-fought restraint. Aakesh, Meetika, and Bob strolled in and sat down.

Naihma raised an eyebrow at Heidi and Chad's seating arrangement, and then went to the front of the room to introduce the guest speaker. Heidi leaned back to find that Chad had put his arm around the back of the chair. At first, this alarmed her, but then she realized how much she enjoyed the way it felt and allowed her body to relax into his. She smelled that fir tree scent again. She'd never realized how much she liked the scent of fir. On some level, she hoped they really were stuck in this chair.

As Naihma spoke the guest's name, Chad's body shook harder. "What does Avinash mean?" he whispered. "Is it hippie for snake oil?"

"It's Indian for indestructible," Avinash declared from the front of the room in a bold, steady voice.

Chad's chest stopped shaking, and his mouth dropped open.

Avinash dramatically pointed to his own ear. "Yoga does remarkable things for one's hearing."

Chad held up a hand. "I apologize.

Sincerely. I'm just finding this all a little overwhelming."

"You are forgiven, fellow traveler," Avinash said.

Chad leaned closer and whispered into Heidi's ear. "Does yoga really help you hear better?"

The feel of his breath on her neck sent goosebumps all the way to her toes. She nodded. "It sure does."

She'd heard Avinash speak many times, and if she was being honest, she'd be content to never hear him speak again. But not tonight. Tonight she wanted him to go on and on. She never wanted to get out of that chair.

Gloria was a non-issue. Chad was every bit the nice guy she'd thought he was earlier in the week. And though there still wasn't really any hope for a future relationship, she could at least enjoy her last few hours with the handsome billionaire, before he went back to his world and left her in hers.

## 27

It was raining on Friday morning. Chad thought this appropriate. Serenity Hills was still a beautiful place, but today there was a somber feel to it. He would be leaving the following morning. Back to the fast lane. This was his last day at Serenity Hills, and though he thought he'd probably come back, knowing his hours were counting down was bittersweet.

Heidi, apparently, sensed only sweetness. No bitterness in sight. "Good morning!" she chirped when he entered the kitchen.

"Where's Bob?" he asked.

"What? I'm not good enough?"

Now *there* was the Heidi he'd known and appreciated earlier in the week.

"You are plenty good enough. I'm just hungry. And you'll just try to feed me herbs."

She smiled. "He'll be right back. He went out to get more chives."

"Chives? What's he doing with chives?"

"Why, he's making cream cheese, of course." She hopped off her stool and headed for the fridge.

"Cream *cheese?* That doesn't sound very non-dairy."

She smiled. "Oh, it is. He makes it out of cashews."

"Yuck!" Some things were meant to be made

of bovine milk. In fact, he couldn't *wait* to have a glass of foamy cow's milk. Chocolate probably. But he wasn't going to tell Heidi that.

She set a bowl out in front of him. "Don't worry. The cashew cheese won't be ready in time for him to try to get you to eat it. But there's this, and it's delicious."

He curled his lip. "It looks like caviar."

She raised an eyebrow. "You don't like caviar? I thought all tycoons liked baby fish."

He snorted. Where had this Heidi been the last few days? "I am not a tycoon, and they are not baby fish. And no, I don't like caviar. Which is weird, because I own a caviar farm."

"They *farm* caviar?"

"Yes, we do. The wild fish population is in danger, and so, we harvest sustainably. We don't even kill the fish."

"What? How's that possible?"

"We surgically remove the eggs and then set mommy fish free to make more."

"What?" she cried, indignant. "That's just as cruel!"

He shrugged. "It's not cruelty-free, but it's less cruel than death. Are you just going to stand there holding that bowl or are you going to feed me?"

She laughed. "Well, I'm not sure what caviar looks like," she said playfully, "but I assure you, there are no fish eggs in Bob's banana mango pudding." As she spoke, she spooned some into a clear glass bowl for him.

Now it looked even more like caviar. "That is not pudding."

"Pudding is a relative term. Just shut up and eat it." She wagged a spoon at him.

*Shut up?* He looked up at her quickly, but her eyes were dancing. He took the spoon and took a bite. She wasn't kidding. It *was* pretty good. Though, it could have used some whipped cream. Actual *cream*. From an actual cow. "No, no, don't put it away," he said, his mouth full. "I'm going to need seconds."

"Take your time. I'll make you some yerba mate."

*My, isn't she being helpful today?* "You're in a good mood."

"I'm always in a good mood."

He had evidence to the contrary, but he stayed silent on the matter.

"So what do you have planned for your last day here?"

Did he hear a hint of sadness in her voice? Would she be sorry to see him go? "That's a good question. I would like to do something special."

The water started to boil, and she turned to pour it into his cup. "You haven't done any yoga. Yoga is special—"

"I did yoga!" He may never have felt more

indignant.

"Okay, you're right. I suppose those two poses count for something. But you really should do more. I don't think you're sold on the practice yet, and I wish you were. It's so good for you, and you can do it at home. It takes very little time or money—" She stopped herself. "Sorry, I'm used to giving this pitch to people who aren't quite as ..." There was a long pause.

"Rich?" he offered.

She let out a breath. "Yeah. Rich."

"You can say it. I'm not embarrassed to be rich. Quite the opposite. I've worked incredibly hard for what I have." What was he doing? Why had he gotten so serious all of a sudden?

"I know that, Chad. I really do. I'll admit, when you got here, I thought that if you were rich, you must've stomped on the backs of others to get that way. But now I know you, and I know you are a genuinely good man. So you don't have to defend your wealth to me. I think the universe blesses those who bless others."

He swallowed. *What?* Who had he blessed?

His question must have shown on his face, because she said, "You know, with all your philanthropy. The elephants, the orphanage, the kids' rec center—"

"Oh yeah," he said, cutting her off. "All that."

"Yeah," she said playfully, leaning toward him over the counter. "*All that*. I love that when I bring it up, you never know what I'm talking about. It's like you forget or something, like you don't even realize how much you do to help others. You're so humble."

His stomach twisted, and he set his spoon down. "So yes. I would love to do some yoga with you."

Her eyes lit up. "Really? Awesome! I can't wait." She set the cup of steaming yerba maté in front of him.

"Yeah. Me neither."


They had to do yoga inside the hut because of the rain. It occurred to Chad that this was a good thing. Part of him still feared Gloria would try to join them again. Maybe if they were out of sight, they'd be out of mind. Or maybe she'd climb a tree and try to watch through the small windows. He kept an eye on them just in case.

He really didn't want to do yoga, but he followed Heidi's instructions. At least—he tried to. He wanted to make her happy, but when he tried to do upward facing dog, his back cried out in protest.

"Don't stretch farther than your body wants to," she said, sensing his distress.

Or maybe he'd whimpered without realizing it.

"Listen to your body."

He listened, but he didn't hear anything helpful. His upward facing dog looked nothing like a dog. It looked like a man lying on the ground and trying, and mostly failing, to look at the ceiling. How had his muscles gotten so tight? He wasn't *that* old! But he had already spent a lifetime at his desk. He vowed to get one of those standing desks when he got back to the office.

"Good! You're doing great!"

*She's either incredibly kind or delusional.* Either way, he loved the sound of her praise. Of course, *she* could do every pose perfectly. She was a yoga master. And wasn't she a beauty while she was at it. He had to look at her in order to mimic what she was doing, but when he looked at her, he found himself admiring the angles and curves of her body a little too closely, and forced himself to look down at his mat.

"Now let's do downward facing dog."

Ugh. He didn't like the sound of that. But he was pleasantly surprised to find this pose easier than the last—except for one small problem. "Am I supposed to be getting dizzy?"

"No! Slowly come out of your current pose and come into a squat ... there ... good ...

good." She spoke calmly and softly. He found it incredibly soothing. "And then lower your head a little and focus on your breathing."

She waited a minute and then asked, "Better?"

"Yeah. Can we stop now?"

"Let's do a few more poses, but I'll go easy on you."


Thirty minutes later, he was surprised to find that he felt amazing. Apparently, contortion agreed with him. She smiled up at him as they walked across the lawn in the light rain. Her smile made his stomach tighten. It was going to be hard to leave this woman. "So, how do you feel?" she asked.

"Like a bendy straw."

She laughed, and it sounded like birdsong. "Excellent. My work is complete."

"I'd like to come back someday. I hope you'll still be here." He opened the door for her, and they both stepped into the dimly lit, dry main building. He breathed in the clove scent. She shook the rain out of her hair, and he got a whiff of flowers. His grandmother had had rose bushes alongside her farmhouse. Heidi's hair smelled like that.

"I would imagine that I'll still be here. I have no plans to go anywhere." She smiled. "Just don't wait too long."

He followed her into the lounge and collapsed on the couch beside her. He realized that he felt more like a wet noodle than a bendy straw.

"So, tell me more about your rec center."

"My rec center?" He sat up straighter.

"Yeah, what do you offer there?"

"Uh ..." This was do or die. He either had to come clean or lie. But he sort of already had lied, right? By omission? So if he came clean now, it would only expose his previous dishonesty. "We have basketball and volleyball."

She made a cute pouty face. "That's it?"

He tried to think of something else a youth center would offer. "Martial arts training. And a pool." This was getting out of hand.

"That sounds better. Do you offer any nutritional training?"

No way would he be able to lie his way through this territory, not with this audience. "Not yet, no."

She nodded thoughtfully. "You really should. You already know enough to help those kids. Teach them about juicing, about the power of raw fruits, and about herbs. You could be even more of a hero!"

*Yeah. Hero.* "It's been fun, Heidi. I appreciate your help, but I think I'm going to hit the showers." He stood to go.

"Oh, okay," she said, her brow furrowed. She let him take a few steps and then said, "Are you all right? I feel like I said something to offend you."

He shook his head vehemently. "Oh no, not at all. I don't think you could offend me if you tried."

## 28

Heidi couldn't stop analyzing her last conversation with Chad. What had gone wrong? What had she said? His mood had turned on a dime. They'd been having so much fun, and then, bam! Sad Chad. She was pretty sure it had happened when she'd asked about the youth center. Maybe he was having trouble there?

She didn't see Chad for that whole afternoon, and then, even though she spent an awkwardly long time in the dining area, she didn't see him around dinner time either. But she couldn't stop thinking about their conversation.

*He must be in his room.* She had to go there. But she couldn't just walk up and knock on his door for a chat. She wasn't Gloria.

She had to come up with an excuse. A reason to knock on his door. She thought for a while, and when the idea came to her, it seemed so simple, she couldn't believe she hadn't thought of it before. She got right to work mixing and matching, making his parting gift.

Twenty minutes later, she knocked on his door softly. All of a sudden her stomach was full of butterflies, and she put a hand over it as if that would calm it down.

He opened the door. "Hey." He didn't sound happy to see her.

"Hey!" She tried to sound bright and cheery, even though the butterflies in her stomach were trying to kill her. "I wasn't sure what time you were leaving tomorrow, and I wanted to give you this essential oil starter kit."

He took the box from her hands and flipped it open. "Wow, that's a lot of oils!"

"Yeah. But you're worth it." Her breath caught. She couldn't believe she'd just said that. She stammered, "I … I … I was thinking you could diffuse some of them in the rec center. They would be so good for the kids. I made you an emotional health blend, an antiviral blend—"

"Thanks." He cut her off. "This is very kind of you." He stepped back as if he was going to shut the door.

"Wait! There are some more oils I'd like to send, to donate to the center. What's the name of the center? I can mail them when I get some more in."

"Oh, you don't have to do that."

"I know that. But I want to." What was wrong with him?

"No really. You've done enough." He started to close the door.

"You seriously won't tell me the name of your rec center?"

He looked as though he didn't feel well.

"Are you feeling all right, Chad? More detox?"

"I'm fine."

She stood there staring at him, trying to decipher his bizarre behavior.

Finally, he said, "It's Rutherford." He looked at the floor. "Rutherford Youth Recreational Facility. Hang on. I'll write down the mailing address." He disappeared into his room and reappeared seconds later with a scrap of paper in his hand. He held it out to her without looking at it—or her.

*What on earth?*

"Thanks." He shut the door, leaving her alone in the hallway with her confusion.

*He is the moodiest man on the planet.* But she knew it was more than that. He wasn't acting *moody*, so much as *guilty.*

With a ball of dread in her stomach, she made her way to the office and was relieved to find it empty. She shook the mouse to wake the old computer up and then typed in the password. The entire staff shared the same password: sanctuary.

She typed Rutherford Youth Recreational Facility into the search box, and nothing came up. She was crushingly disappointed, but she wasn't really surprised. She added "Boston" to the name and tried again. Still nothing.

She thought about typing in the mailing address he'd just handed her, but it was a P.O. box.

She tried Chad LaChance elephants and Chad LaChance orphanage. Nada. She was out of hope. She tried Chad LaChance philanthropy, and found an article from a local Massachusetts newspaper criticizing him for never supporting any charities. She started to read it, but couldn't make herself finish. She closed the window and left the room, her eyes wet with tears.

She was so disappointed, but she was also furious. She was mad at him for lying, and at herself for being so gullible. Boy, he had fooled her good. He really was just a rich, selfish jerk. Thank goodness she hadn't allowed herself to fall for him, or to get involved. What a mess that would have made. Thank goodness she had kept her distance.

She ran into Gloria in the hallway and quickly wiped at her eyes to get rid of the evidence. "Hey, Gloria," she said, trying to keep her voice level.

"Hey what?"

Heidi stopped walking. "You remember when you told us about Chad's philanthropy?"

"Huh?"

"You know, the elephants? The orphanage? You told us all about his generosity one night while we were eating."

She folded her arms across her chest and pursed her lips. "I have absolutely no idea what you're talking about."

*Wow.* Heidi didn't know what to say, so she walked away. Chad and Gloria were both destructive liars. She couldn't wait for them to go home. They were the worst guests Serenity Hills had ever had.

## 29

Chad knew who it was from the sound of her footsteps. He groaned, rolled over in bed, and pulled the covers up over his head, as if that could stop the confrontation that was coming.

Why had he made up a stupid name? He'd known she'd look it up, because he'd acted so suspiciously. So why didn't he pick a generic name? The Boston Youth Center? There had to be one of those. But no, he'd said Rutherford. His grandmother's maiden name. He had never been a liar. Now he found himself wishing he'd had more practice over the course of his life. Because he was certainly bad at it.

She pounded on the door. He didn't do anything, not because he wanted to ignore her or thought he *could* ignore her, but because he didn't know how to respond. What was he going to say to her? He had never been so ashamed in his whole life.

She knocked again. Then she wiggled the doorknob. Of course, his door was locked, though she wasn't necessarily the one he was trying to keep out.

"Chad! I know you're in there! Open the stupid door!"

He had never heard her sound so angry. He was actually a little afraid of her in this moment. He forced himself out of bed, trudged to the door, and opened it. Then he held up a hand. "Please, don't. I know what you're going to say. I'm sorry."

"You're *sorry*? That's it? Why on earth would you lie to me like that? I thought we were friends!" Her eyes were wet, her voice pitched high enough to crack glass.

"To be fair, I didn't make up the lie. Then when you were so impressed, I didn't have the heart to tell you that I wasn't as impressive as you thought."

"What?" She looked confused.

"I never told anyone that I had adopted elephants. That's ridiculous. I'm not even creative enough to think of such a thing. And it's not like I've been squandering my fortune. I invested all my money back into my business. I'm trying to grow. And my business helps people. So you can think whatever you want to think of me, and I'm sorry that I lied to you, but I didn't mean to." He was feeling a little angry himself, and this made him feel better. Anger felt far better than shame.

She stepped into his room. Her eyes searched him.

He felt vulnerable, a feeling he wasn't used to.

"You had ample opportunity to set me straight." She took a step closer to him. She was only inches away, looking up into his eyes. She lowered her voice. "So why didn't you set me straight?"

"I told you. You seemed so happy to think those things about me. I didn't want to disappoint you."

"So you lied? You lied to me? You've disappointed me far more by lying than you would have by telling me you didn't have any elephants."

He couldn't help it. He chuckled. It was obvious she did not appreciate that. But he and his health coach were fighting over elephants. If that wasn't funny, he didn't know what was. She opened her mouth to holler at him again, and he couldn't take it anymore. Without thinking he wrapped his arm around her waist and pulled her to him. Then he gently placed his lips on hers. He hesitated, their mouths barely touching, as he waited to see how she would react. But she didn't pull away. Her arm went around his waist and her fingers climbed his back, sending shivers up his spine. His whole head was tingling. Her lips parted slightly, and he deepened the kiss. She responded in kind, and he thought maybe he had died and gone to heaven. He had kissed a few women in his day, but he had never kissed anyone like this. Her lips were made for his. And he never wanted to stop kissing them.

All at once, she pulled away. "I'm sorry. I can't—" She turned and fled, leaving him alone with his head spinning and his skin still tingling.

## 30

It had been the kiss of all kisses, even better than their first. Heidi crawled into bed thinking about it. She lay awake most of the night, unable to sleep because she couldn't stop thinking about it. When she did finally fall asleep, she dreamt about it, and when she woke to the sunlight streaming through her window, that kiss was the first thing she thought of. She put her fingers to her lips, remembering the feel of his skin on hers.

His lips were as soft as flower petals, and they tasted like cinnamon. That kiss had awoken every fiber of her being. She had lost herself in that kiss, and she hadn't wanted it to stop. But then she'd stopped it.

She shouldn't have been kissing Chad LaChance. He was way out of her league, and even if he wasn't—he'd proven to be untrustworthy. She didn't need a friend like that, let alone a partner. She had no interest in kissing someone just for the sake of kissing him. If intimacy wasn't heading toward relationship, then she wasn't interested.

She heard tires crunching over the gravel driveway and sat up in bed. She'd slept in on purpose so that he'd be gone when she got up, but she hadn't slept long enough, apparently, because there was the Uber. She watched the blue sedan pull up to the front of the house and the driver get out nervously. But he didn't have to go to the door, because there was Chad, wearing a pressed dress shirt, stone-colored slacks, and shiny leather shoes. She hadn't seen him dressed like that since he arrived. She much preferred the T-shirt, cargo shorts, and flip-flops version of Chad.

He wheeled his suitcase down the walkway toward the car, carrying something else under his arm. He put the suitcase in the trunk, and when he slammed it shut, she saw that he was still holding the box of oils she'd given him. *Well, isn't that sweet?* He was going to keep her gift with him for the drive. Or maybe he didn't want the girly-smelling oils to spill in his thousand dollar suitcase. She didn't know if suitcases could cost that much, but she thought probably.

Chad reached for the car door's handle and then paused. He looked longingly back at the house, and for a moment, their eyes met. She ducked beneath the windowsill and then pulled the covers over her head for good measure. Just in case he had a long distance periscope. She groaned. She'd been caught staring at him from her bed at ten o'clock. She was so mortified. Why not suffer one last final indignity? It had become par for the course. As she lay there in hiding, waiting to hear the Uber drive away, she heard a high pitched "Wait!"

She raised her head the minimum amount needed to peek over the windowsill and saw Gloria running down the walkway dragging a hot pink suitcase behind her.

Chad climbed back out of the car, looking exasperated. "What?" She couldn't hear his voice, but she could read his lips. Those beautiful, miraculous lips.

Gloria had closed the gap between predator and prey. She let go of the suitcase and began to gesticulate wildly. Chad calmly shook his head. Heidi couldn't really blame him for not wanting to share a two-hour Uber ride with his stalker. Gloria took a step closer to him, but Chad stood his ground. He shook his head and then turned and climbed back into the car. And then both she and Gloria watched as the most interesting man Heidi had ever known drove out of their lives. And the way Heidi had allowed things to end, he was probably out of her life for good.

After a few more minutes of lying there feeling sorry for herself, she forced herself out of bed. She showered, got dressed, and then stood in front of the mirror. She was adamant about her daily affirmations, but today she struggled to find the words.

She looked her reflection in the eye and said, "He was not a part of your life plan. He was not a part of your goals. His plans do not match yours. His goals do not align with yours. He was just a blip on the radar of your life, and soon he will be a fading memory."

She took a deep breath and let it out slowly, trying to push her feelings for the billionaire out with the air. There. She felt better. And as she headed to the kitchen for sustenance, most of the normal bounce in her step had returned.

"Hiya, Bob!"

He looked up from his cutting board, his brows raised in skepticism. "Aren't we chipper? Sleeping in must be good for the mood."

"It's a beautiful day in the neighborhood, Bob!" She grabbed a banana and started peeling it as she sat down on one of the stools. She took a big bite, and then said, "Won't you be my neighbor?" She winked.

"You're overcompensating."

She swallowed and took another bite. "Am not." There was no use pretending she didn't know what he was talking about. She shouldn't have come to the kitchen. Bob was really messing with her qi.

He leaned on the counter and looked at her. "I'm sorry it didn't work out. I know you guys had a special connection."

She swallowed. "We really didn't, Bob. Honestly. There's nothing to be sorry for."

He stood straight and flipped the towel he was holding over his shoulder. "We've been friends a long time, Heidi. I'm not sure why you feel you need to lie to me, but you do what you gotta do."

Heidi threw away the banana peel and then grabbed another banana for the road. She turned to go.

"It's still not too late," he called after her.

"It was too late before it started," she called back. She wasn't even sure if that would make sense to Bob, but it made sense to her.

## 31

Chad sat in his conference room as his Chief Financial Officer shared his report. He knew he was supposed to be listening, but instead, he was staring out the giant bay window that looked out over Boston Harbor and thinking about Heidi.

It had been three weeks since he'd left Serenity Hills, so why was he still so hung up on her? He'd been fond of her, sure. And he'd enjoyed being around her. He was attracted to her, and given different circumstances, that attraction could have blossomed into something much grander, but his current circumstances were not those.

He'd been so certain when he left that hippie compound that his feelings for his health coach would fade away as the days went by.

They hadn't. He was having trouble sleeping, because he couldn't stop thinking about her. Even though he'd been dousing his pillow with the lavender oil she'd so graciously donated to his make-believe children in need, he couldn't seem to nod off without tossing and turning for hours first. Thus, he would wake exhausted in the morning. And after several days of trying to combat such fatigue with yerba maté, he had switched back to coffee, and as wonderful as it tasted to his deprived taste buds, he felt guilty with every sip.

When he drank coffee, he thought of Heidi. When he smelled flowers, he thought of Heidi. When he drank juice, he thought of Heidi. When he sat sweating in his sauna, he thought of Aakesh. But everything else was Heidi. He dreamt about her at night. He daydreamed about her during the day. He often wondered what she was doing. What was she doing right now? What man was she coaching back to health, and was that man doing a better job of winning her heart than he had?

Wait. What? Where had that thought come from?

His CFO snapped his fingers. "Earth to Chad. You in there?"

"Yeah, yeah, Matt. I'm in here." Chad looked at his team. Everyone in the room was staring at him.

"I know you came back from that health resort slim and trim and hooked on parsley juice," Matt said, "but your brain hasn't been right since. You're distracted. Off your game. Frankly, I'm wondering if you didn't leave your brain back there. Maybe you should go get it."

Several people laughed. Chad didn't. "I think you're right. I did leave something behind at Serenity Hills." He pushed his chair back from the table. "And I need to go get it. If you'll excuse me, we'll finish this meeting when I get back."

"You've got to be kidding!" Matt cried. "What do we do until then?"

"I trust you to keep the ship afloat till I get back. I won't be long." He left the conference room, shutting the door behind him so they could talk behind his back. He didn't even blame them. He was acting out of character. He loosened his tie as he walked down the hallway.

"Brenda, can you please ask Steve to bring the car around? I need to go to the apartment. And also, tell Alec to get my plane ready. We're going back to Augusta, Maine. And get me a rental car when I get there. I'm not taking another Uber."

Her eyes grew wider as he talked, and she scribbled notes down on a pad.

"Thank you, Brenda. I appreciate it."

He stabbed at the elevator button with extra oomph. Now that he'd made his mind up, his heart was filled with a sense of urgency. Why had he waited so long?

His heart rate didn't slow until his plane was off the ground, and then he finally relaxed and leaned back in his plush leather seat. He eyed the minibar. He usually had a drink on his plane, but he hadn't touched alcohol since he'd been back. He'd sort of lost his taste for it, but right now he was tempted. The truth was, he was a little nervous about seeing Heidi again. What would she say? What would she think? Was he acting like a stalker? Was he being a Gloria? And Heidi had been *so* mad at him when he'd left. And she had every right to be. He'd lied to her. He couldn't even believe he'd done it. He wasn't a liar. He didn't know if he could ever win her trust back.

He reclined his seat and closed his eyes. He had to stop analyzing the situation. Whatever would happen would happen. He would tell Heidi how he felt, and if she was happy to hear it, then great. If she wasn't, then that was great too. Because then he could get on with his life and stop obsessing over his hippie health coach. But he really hoped she would be happy to hear what he had to say.

The flight from Boston to Augusta was less than an hour. It seemed like an eternity.

## 32

Heidi was trying to enjoy a bowl of arugula salad when she noticed Bob was staring at her. She looked up, a small piece of lettuce sticking out of her mouth. She sucked it in, chewed, swallowed, and said, "What?"

Then she realized Naihma had appeared from nowhere and was standing on her left side. She looked at Naihma. "What?"

A gentle hand on her back made her look to her right to see Fawsa. Her stomach sank. "What's going on?"

Fawsa opened her mouth, but Naihma interrupted her. "Wait a second. Aakesh and Meetika will be here soon."

"Are we having a family meeting?" Heidi asked.

Fawsa began to rub her back. It felt amazing, even though Naihma was the resident masseuse.

"Yes," Naihma said, in a soft voice Heidi recognized. It was the one she used with terminally ill guests. "In a moment."

"In the kitchen?" Heidi looked around to make sure she was really in the kitchen. This whole scenario was so bizarre, she feared she was missing something obvious.

"We can go into the lounge if it would make you more comfortable."

Make *her* more comfortable? Why was her comfort the main goal? Why was her comfort even on the goal sheet?

"Sorry we're late," a deep voice boomed from the doorway. "Did you start without us?"

"No, Aakesh. We're waiting for Heidi to finish her salad," Naihma said, "and then we're all going to the lounge."

Heidi pushed her delicious meal away from her. Something had spoiled her appetite. "I'm finished."

A guest entered the room and started when he saw all the people. "Sorry, am I interrupting something?" Elijah was a seventeen-year-old skateboarder from New York City. His parents had sent him to Serenity Hills to get some fresh air, and in hopes that he'd forget about his new girlfriend. She was all he talked about. Heidi sincerely doubted the parents' plan would work. She didn't have an herb to get rid of teenage love.

Bob looked at Naihma. "Go ahead. I'll get Elijah some nourishment and then I'll be in."

Naihma nodded stoically and turned to leave the room. Fawsa took Heidi's hand in hers, which alarmed Heidi. They were friendly, but they weren't really hand-holding friendly. She remembered Chad saying that Gloria had forced him to hold her hand, and the memory made her head reel and her stomach turn.

She was so *sick* of thinking about Chad. Why couldn't she just forget about him? It wasn't for lack of trying.

A horrible theory crossed her mind then. Was that what this family meeting was about? Chad? She looked around at the familiar faces settling into the lounge furniture. Surely not. They wouldn't call a family meeting because she was heartsick for a man she hardly knew, a liar of a man she shouldn't be missing.

"Heidi," Naihma began, "we are here together, unified in spirit, to try to help you."

"This is your intervention," Aakesh said. Naihma had sat in a chair across from Heidi and was leaning forward toward her. Fawsa had sat beside Heidi and resumed the back rubbing. Meetika was on the floor, her legs folded beneath her, looking up at Heidi with care in her eyes. But Aakesh was still standing with his arms folded across his chest, looking down at her domineeringly.

Naihma shot him a scolding look.

When Heidi saw that, she allowed herself to glare at him too. He could be really annoying.

"I *said* we weren't going to use that word," Naihma said.

Aakesh shrugged. "Sorry." His tone was void of remorse. "It is what it is."

Heidi had always hated that expression, even more so now.

Naihma looked at Heidi. "We are not here to try to manipulate you, but we love you, and we are afraid that you are living a truth you are unaware of. So we are here to speak truth into your life."

Heidi wished they would get on with it, whatever *it* was. "What?" Heidi said again.

Naihma reached out and placed a hand on Heidi's knee. "Honey, you are in love with Chad LaChance."

Heidi gasped. "What?!" How rude! They had no idea the state of her heart, and she was certainly not *in love* with that lying jerk. "He's a lying jerk!" she cried.

"I told them you'd say that," Bob said from the doorway. He crossed the room and sat on the other side of Heidi. She wondered if she was going to get two backrubs. Bob had been her only confidant in the last three weeks, and now she regretted sharing anything with him. He'd sold her out. She glared at him too.

"Don't be angry with him," Naihma said softly. "He didn't say anything out of turn. None of us know the details of your situation, but the basic premise is obvious to us all. Your heart is broken."

"My *heart* is my *business*," Heidi said through clenched teeth. She knew it wasn't healthy to hold her jaw so tight, so she forced it to relax, and added, "And my heart is *not* broken."

"I told them you'd say that too."

Bob may not have "spoken out of turn," but it was obvious he had spoken plenty. Far more than she had wanted him to. She vowed to never speak to him again.

"Heidi," Meetika said in a voice so quiet Heidi had to lean in to hear her. "For the last three weeks, you've been living sans spark. You've lost your mojo. Your qi is blocked—"

"What she's trying to say," Aakesh interrupted, "is that you've been cranky, lazy, and just generally unpleasant to be around since you watched the billionaire drive away."

She started. For a couple of reasons. First, how did he know she'd watched Chad leave? That was downright creepy. And second, *had* she been cranky, lazy, or unpleasant? She hadn't thought so. She didn't want to be those things, and had *never* been accused of being those things.

"I'm sorry." Heidi looked around the small group. "I didn't realize I was being so obnoxious. I'll do better." Her tone sounded ironic. She wasn't sure if she'd meant to be ironic or not.

Naihma took her literally. "No, no dear. You're not being obnoxious. That's not what we're saying at all—"

"And we're going to stop you before you get

to obnoxiousville." Bob held up a keyring and jingled some keys at her.

"What?" Heidi said again.

"I'm driving you to Boston. You are going to declare your love to your soulmate." Bob raised his eyebrows and looked like a cocky professor. "I am confident he will reciprocate your feelings. But even if for some crazy reason he won't be excited to receive your affection, at least you'll have done what you can, and then you can get on with your life."

Heidi looked at Bob, and then at Naihma. She was incredulous. "I can't go declare my love for a billionaire I hardly know. You guys are nuts!"

"No," Bob said. "What's nuts is moping around here like a zombie. You love the guy. We know it, and on some level, you know it. I'm sorry he lied to you, but in the great scheme of things, so what? Get over it! You're the most forgiving person I've ever met, so what's different about this guy? Go pack a bag, because I don't want to drive down and back in one day. We'll find someplace to spend the night."

Heidi couldn't imagine riding all the way to Boston, let alone trying to get *around* Boston, in Bob's ancient VW Beetle. "And if I refuse?"

"Then you're fired," Naihma declared.

Heidi's jaw dropped. "What?"

Naihma nodded. "Fired. Canned. Adios."

In a different emotional atmosphere, this would have been funny, but Heidi was anything but amused. "You can't be serious."

"I am not joking, Heidi. This is no laughing matter. I can't imagine why, because I thought you were a wiser soul than this, but you are punishing yourself. We are in the health business here, and that is incredibly unhealthy. So, do what Bob says, and go work things out with your man."

"I totally think you should work things out. Love is important, man."

Heidi looked up to see Elijah standing in the doorway, still eating his arugula salad.

Heidi stood up abruptly. "Fine!" she said, because she didn't know what else to say. "But, I'm not letting Bob go with me. I'll take the bus." She tried to stomp off, slowing to step over Meetika's legs.

"How are you going to get to the bus station?" Bob asked, jingling his keys again.

It was a reasonable question. The closest bus station was over an hour away. She turned back. "Bob, could I please have a ride to the bus terminal?" she asked, her words clipped.

"Why sure, Heidi! I aim to please!" he said with excessive exuberance.

Annoyed, she continued her angry exit from

the room.

Halfway to her bedroom, she realized she was still stomping, and forced a lighter step. It wasn't her knees' fault that her coworkers had lost their collective mind.

It didn't take her long to pack. She didn't have the mental capacity to even do it logically. She threw a bunch of random stuff in a backpack and headed outside, where she found Bob waiting by his ridiculous car. She fell into the front seat and slammed the door.


The bus station was *packed.* Heidi couldn't imagine why so many people were in Waterville, Maine, nor why they were all trying to get out at the same time.

"Why don't I stick around until you have a ticket in hand?" Bob looked at her, one eyebrow raised. "To be on the safe side."

She navigated toward the ticket counter, stepping over legs, charging electronics, and rucksacks, and weaving between standing couples. She had to stand in line for twenty minutes to learn that the next available seat to Boston would be at eleven o'clock that night. She did not want to hang out at the bus station for that long. She did not want to hang out in Waterville, Maine that long. Waterville did have a restaurant that made the best vegan sushi she'd ever had, but even she couldn't eat sushi for nine hours.

She stepped back out into the bright sunshine, and found Bob right where she'd left him. She climbed into the car, rested her elbow on the window frame, leaned back, and said, "Bob, would you please take me to Boston?"

"I would like nothing more," Bob said, and turned the key. Nothing happened.

Heidi groaned.

He turned the key again. Still nothing.

"Third time's a charm," Bob declared and tried again. This time the car sprang to life. "See? I told you!"

Thus began a very long, very hairy travel experience. But despite several near-death encounters, Bob did get her to the address Naihma had provided. Heidi still couldn't believe her boss had just given up Chad's personal info like that. They all better hope he would be happy to see her, or they could be facing a lawsuit, and she highly doubted Serenity Hills could keep up with Chad LaChance's lawyers.

And the truth was, she *didn't* think he'd be happy to see her. The closer to Boston they got, the more honest Heidi tried to be with herself. She obviously *did* have feelings for Chad. She'd only been kidding herself when she'd pretended otherwise.

But he was still a big city billionaire. How could such a relationship possibly work? Surely Chad, if he even *was* interested in her romantically, would be pragmatic enough to see that such a pairing wouldn't work. Besides, she hadn't been too nice to him before he'd left. If that's how he remembered her, this was going to be a wasted trip. Well, maybe not *completely* wasted, as it would at least satisfy her meddling coworkers.

They pulled onto a long tar drive. The old elm trees on either side of the road reached up and over the road, so Heidi felt as though she was driving through a tunnel. Claustrophobia began to press in, and she focused on her breathing.

"I don't know if the house is old, but his driveway sure is," Bob said, looking up at the treetops admiringly.

"Keep your eyes on the road, please. It would be very embarrassing to get into an accident in his driveway."

They came to a large metal gate, and her anxiety increased.

"It's all good. Don't worry," Bob said.

She wasn't convinced.

Bob gave the gate several seconds to open on its own, and then rolled down his window to press a button on a squawk box.

"How can I help you?" a male voice asked. He sounded tough. Heidi pictured a burly bodyguard throwing them both out into the street.

"Maybe we should turn around," she said through almost closed lips. *Who does this? Who just drives up to a billionaire's front gate?*

"I have Heidi Leeman here to see Chad LaChance." Apparently, Heidi Leeman does. That's who.

"Stand by please."

They waited awkwardly. She imagined his security team looking at them on video, and wondering why anyone would drive such a vehicle. The running engine sounded exceptionally loud in the stillness. Heidi was worried it was going to blow up and die right there in the billionaire's driveway. The perfect cherry on top of the embarrassment cake.

"I'm sorry," the voice came back. "We are unable to reach Mr. LaChance at the moment. He must be out of cellular range."

## 33

This trip north differed from Chad's last one. Mile by mile, as he drew closer to the Maine forest, he felt he was getting closer to home. It wasn't that he didn't love Boston. He did. That was his hometown, the city where all his dreams had come true, and he didn't want to leave there, ever. But now he had a different dream, and he couldn't believe he hadn't allowed himself to truly dream it before.

Heidi. Why had he waited so long? What might have happened if he'd declared his feelings for her in the horseshoe pit? Or on the garden porch swing? Or heaven forbid—the yoga shack? He smirked as he silently corrected himself—the yoga *hut*.

The scenery seemed more beautiful this trip. Or maybe he just had a better view from the driver's seat. Or maybe, this time, he was seeing the mountains through the eyes of someone in love. He couldn't wait to see her. Her hair that looked like sunshine. Her eyes that danced. He couldn't wait to smell her lilac skin. He shook his head and forced himself to focus on the traffic, or he'd accidentally get funneled into one of Maine's many tourist traps.

Finally, he got off the interstate, and the traffic thinned to a trickle. He weaved his way through the woods until he seemed to be the only car on the road.

He recognized the turn before his GPS even told him to take it. The long dirt road that would lead to Serenity Hills. He took the turn and forced himself to slow down. He was no expert at driving on gravel roads, but he was fairly certain one wasn't supposed to go eighty miles per hour on them.

He breathed a sigh of relief when the driveway, and the small, nearly illegible sign announcing Serenity Hills, came into view. "Welcome to Serenity Hills—where peace reigns." The nerves started. What would she think? Should he have called first? He looked down at what he was wearing. He'd taken off his jacket, but he was still wearing the rest of his suit. He loosened his tie and then decided to rip it off altogether. He tossed it in the backseat, wishing he'd changed his clothes before he left. She was going to think he was a tool. He shook his head to clear his thoughts, and the massage hut came into view. He turned a corner and more buildings popped into view including the sauna, which had no steam pouring out of it today. And then there was the art studio, and his favorite—the yoga hut. He smiled at the memory.

He pulled into the small parking lot and tried to look cool as he strolled up the walkway—in case anyone was watching. He paused at the door, wondering if he should knock, and then decided against it. He opened the door and walked in as if that was the most natural thing in the world. The smell of cloves greeted him, and he was overwhelmed by that comfortable feeling one gets when he first enters his home after a long trip away.

There was no one in the foyer. He made his way to the lounge, where the clove smell gave way to cinnamon. Still no one. He went to the kitchen, where a teenager stood with a skateboard under his arm and his head in the fridge. Chad wondered where he was going to skateboard at Serenity Hills.

"Excuse me," Chad said.

Slowly, the teen turned. He had a glass serving bowl full of something green and red in his hand.

Chad's mouth watered. Apparently, he missed Bob's food more than he thought.

"Sup, dude?"

Chad chuckled. "Do you know where Bob is?"

"Who's Bob?"

Chad looked at the bowl. "The chef who made what's in your hand."

Skateboard kid looked down at the food. Then he set the bowl on the island. "Oh. Uh, he went for a road trip, I guess."

A road trip? "Okay, do you know where Heidi is?"

Mr. Unhelpful reached in and grabbed a handful of food.

Chad considered telling him where the utensils were.

He filled his mouth, and then, chewing loudly, said, "No idea who Heidi is, dude."

Chad gave up then and left the kitchen. Where was everybody? Had skateboard kid scared them all off?

He checked the office, rechecked the lounge, and then decided to head out to the garden. Maybe Heidi was in their favorite porch swing. He opened the front door to leave, and Aakesh nearly fell through the doorway.

"Ah! Sorry. I was in a hurry to get in." He looked up, and his eyes widened with recognition. "What are you doing here?" He didn't sound pleased to see him.

Chad chose to ignore the rudeness. "I'm looking for Heidi."

A look of realization appeared on Aakesh's face. "Uh oh."

"What?"

"Heidi's not here. She went to Boston. To find *you*."

The words took Chad's breath away. She'd done what? "How long ago?"

Aakesh looked around the foyer, as if looking for a clock, but there weren't any. "I'm not sure. Maybe four hours ago?"

"I need to use your phone. Right now."

## 34

"Oh wait," the squawk box said. "I guess we just heard from him. Come on in."

The gate began its slow swing open, and Heidi looked at Bob in terror. "I guess there's no going back now."

Bob drove slowly up the picturesque drive, and soon a mansion came into view. Heidi's breath caught. It looked to be about the size of five normal houses. The driveway curled around a large fountain that sprayed water into the air, casting a rainbow over his front doors.

As Bob grew closer to the house, a man and a woman hurried out. The man was enormous. The woman was tiny. They made a funny pair. But despite the discrepancy in size, they moved at the same speed, a speed that made Heidi nervous. Why were they in such a tizzy? They walked toward the car, and Heidi began to wonder if they were going to grab it as they drove by, but Bob stopped before she could find out. The man went to Bob's door, and the woman came to Heidi's.

Mr. Muscles opened Bob's door. "Welcome! Welcome! Come right in. We'll have someone park the car."

*What is going on? What's with the overly enthusiastic welcome party?* The woman opened Heidi's door. "Are you Heidi?" She didn't give Heidi a chance to answer. "Yes, of course you are. Come right this way. I'm Phoebe, Mr. LaChance's personal assistant, and I'll take good care of you till he gets back."

"Gets back? When will that be?"

Phoebe was already on her way up the steps and didn't answer her. Heidi looked over her shoulder to see if Bob was coming, and he was, though he looked like he was auditioning for a *Honey, I Shrunk the Kids* sequel next to his new friend. Heidi turned and followed Phoebe, who was holding the front door open.

Heidi stepped into a grand front hall. Gleaming hardwood floors led to a wide staircase. Heidi looked up to see a balcony that stretched around three of the walls.

"Right this way," Phoebe said, and led her to their right, through another set of double doors, and into a large, gorgeously decorated living room.

Everything was done in maroon and yellow, which had a powerful effect. The maroon felt warm, comforting, and inviting, while the pops of yellow cheered her, and seemed to bring energy to the room. "Wowsa. This is beautiful."

"Oh yes, it was designed by Agatha Arnold."

Heidi looked at Bob, who looked as wide-eyed as she felt. She wasn't sure how she was supposed to respond to such random information, so she didn't say anything.

"Oh, sorry," Phoebe said quickly. "I forgot you're from Maine."

*Oh sure, it was geography that prevented me from knowing who Agatha Arnold is.* And how did Phoebe know she was from Maine? Oh duh, Chad had probably just told them on the phone. Suddenly, she was overwhelmed with a longing for him. She was standing in his gorgeous house, but she only wanted *him.*

Phoebe was still talking. "... the best interior designer in Boston. She's in high demand, but Mr. LaChance was able to get her, of course."

"Of course," Heidi said, because she didn't know what else to say. When in Rome, just agree with the Romans. "Well, it's lovely. Do you know when Chad will be back?"

Phoebe deftly dodged the question. "We have a large-screen TV, surround sound ..."

Heidi looked around the room, but there was no sign of a television.

"It's concealed right now, but I can get it ready for you if you'd like to watch television. Are you hungry or thirsty? I could have some food prepared or brought in? And we have a fully stocked bar." She nodded toward a bar in the corner.

The bodyguard hadn't followed them into the room, and Heidi realized that Phoebe was completely ignoring Bob. "Are you hungry, Bob?"

"No, thank you." His tone made it clear he understood why she'd asked.

"Or, if you prefer," Phoebe continued, "I could show you to the spa—"

"He has a *spa* in his house?" Wonders never ceased.

A small giggle escaped Phoebe's lips, which made her seem less robotic. "I know it's a little strange. Mr. LaChance never uses it, but it was here when he bought the home, so he keeps it for guests. We also have an indoor pool? Or an outdoor one if you prefer."

Heidi had no desire to swim at that moment, but for some reason, she said, "I didn't bring a swimsuit."

"Oh, we can get you one," Phoebe said quickly.

Heidi held up both hands. "No, no, that's okay." She just wanted Chad. "We can wait here. He *is* coming, right?"

Phoebe nodded. "He's on his way."

"You okay with watching some TV, Bob?"

"Yeah. That would be great. Do you have on demand streaming? I'm suddenly in the mood for some *Downton Abbey*."

Heidi snickered.

"Absolutely." Phoebe crossed the room in several quick steps, and pulled a remote control out of a drawer. She pressed a button, and doors on the wall slid open to reveal a giant flat-screen TV.

"What's that measure, 100 inches?" Heidi quipped.

"One hundred and ten," Phoebe said.

The theater-sized screen blinked on, and Phoebe handed Heidi the remote. "Here you go. Make yourself comfortable. Let me know if you need anything. I'll be right outside." She turned to go.

"Uh, about that food. Do you have any fruit?" Bob asked.

"Yes, some fruit would be lovely," Heidi added, because she wasn't sure Bob would get any food unless she pretended to want it too.

"Of course. Any kind of fruit in particular?"

"I never met a fruit I didn't like," Bob said.

She nodded. "All right then. I'll bring you a variety. Be back shortly."

She disappeared, and Bob fell back into the plush sectional. "I can't even *imagine* living like this," he said, sprawling his limbs out in all directions.

"I know." Heidi sat down gently. She was scared to move in this room, afraid she'd break something. "I feel like I'm on a different planet."

## 35

Upon Chad's urging, Steve broke every speed limit between the airport and home. When he finally pulled up in front of the steps, Chad jumped out and jogged up the steps.

"They're in there," Phoebe said, pointing. She looked relieved to be rid of her charge. He *had* threatened to fire her if they left.

"Thanks, Phoebe. Sorry if I was a bear on the phone."

She nodded stoically and vanished.

He flung open the door and then laughed out loud. The sight of her filled his heart with joy that bubbled up and out his throat. Also, Bob lay sound asleep on his couch, with his feet up on his incredibly expensive coffee table, right next to a tray full of melon rinds. Phoebe had taken good care of them, just as he'd asked.

Heidi stood when she saw him. He crossed the room, and all the rehearsed declarations, all the perfect things he was going to say, fled his brain. So he abandoned language and simply went to her.

As he closed the gap, Heidi stepped toward him. He got a whiff of lilacs, and smiled as he breathed in the refreshing scent. He reached out and took her hands, but then immediately dropped them as he wrapped his arms around her instead. He placed his lips on hers, barely touching her at first, as if asking for permission, which she quickly gave as she pressed her body into his. He stopped holding back then, and kissed her like he meant it, like he'd been waiting his whole life to kiss her.

"Should I leave?"

Chad pulled away from the kiss to avoid laughing in her face, and looked down at Bob. "Yeah, Bob. It's nice to see you, but that would be great. Go ahead and explore."

"Do you have a bowling alley?"

Chad scowled. "Uh, no. But there's a hot tub in the spa. Make yourself at home."

Bob, looking reluctant, peeled himself off the couch, winked at Heidi, and then left the room.

Chad sat down in the spot Bob had just vacated, and pulled Heidi down beside him.

"I'm sorry," she said, her voice trembling.

"You have *nothing* to be sorry for. I'm the one who lied, and you can't imagine how much I wish I hadn't. I just couldn't believe how it made me feel when you were impressed with me, when you thought I was some generous elephant dad."

She giggled. "I'm still impressed with you." She looked around the room. "This place is so beautiful."

He slid closer to her. "Nothing is as beautiful as you. I'm pretty sure I loved you the first time

I met you. I'm so sorry it took me so long to figure that out. And then once I did figure it out, I'm so sorry it took me so long to find the courage to tell you. I love you, Heidi."

She let out a long breath, and it sounded shaky. Her eyes were sparkling. "I didn't think I could love you because you're rich." She glanced down at their hands and then looked back up into his eyes. "Isn't that silly? I don't care if you're rich or poor. I just want to be with you. I love you, Chad. Even if you are a big, bad Boston billionaire."

He took another deep breath. That was his cue. "I love Boston, Heidi, but I don't have to live here. I can run my business from Maine if you want me to. All I care about is being near you."

Heidi smiled up at him, and a warmth filled him all the way to his toes. If there had been any remaining doubts about his feelings for her, they vanished with that smile. "I can't believe you just said that, and it means a lot that you did, but I came here to tell you that I can move here. If you want me to."

His heart leapt. "Really? Because I had an amazing idea." He took a deep breath and squeezed her hands. "At least, *I* think it's an amazing idea." He laughed awkwardly. "If you don't think it's amazing, that's okay. Anyway, no pressure, but there is a recreational center in Lincolntown that's been closed for nearly two years. I would like to buy it. I would like to be the man you believed I could be. But, I would need someone to run the center." He paused, searching her eyes. "Do you think you'd be up for such a job?"

Her eyes filled with tears. "I think I was *born* for such a job."

He had never felt so full, so hopeful, so happy. He gently put his hands to her cheeks and pulled her toward his lips, and he tried to show her the fullness of his heart with that kiss.

She pulled away a little and looked into his eyes. "I have one question."

"Yes?"

"Where are we going to keep the elephants?"

# Epilogue

Heidi tried to be patient as Steve battled Boston traffic to get her to the youth center. It was completely her fault she was running late, but she wished Steve would work a little harder at making up the time. After nearly two years, she still hadn't gotten used to being driven around by a professional.

Finally, he stopped the car in front of the entrance. She hopped out without letting him get out to open the door. "Thanks, Steve," she called as she ran inside.

"Hey, Jeremiah!" She high-fived the twelve-year-old who was hanging around the door. "You okay?"

"Yeah. I was looking to see if my uncle was here. He said he'd come to watch my game. But he's late. Again."

"Uncle Mac?"

Jeremiah nodded, his face long.

"I bet he'll be here. Does Coach know where you are?"

Jeremiah looked at the floor and shook his head.

"Why don't you go back to the gym then. I promise that when your uncle gets here, I'll make sure he finds you."

Jeremiah ran off, and she followed him into the gym. She looked up into the bleachers and was happy to see at least a few fans had shown up for the game. This wasn't always the case.

She walked down the sideline. "Hey, Coach! How are things looking?"

Chad turned toward her. His face lit up, and he leaned in for a kiss. "Things always look awesome whenever you're around."

"Awww!" She never tired of his sweet talk.

He lovingly rubbed her belly. "How are you feeling?"

"Was a little sick this morning, but I'm getting better every day. I got some more decorations for the nursery today!" She could practically already hear the pitter patter of little feet in the mansion. She hadn't realized how much she wanted a child until she had one in her belly.

He laughed. "Ever since you decided on a theme, you haven't wasted any time."

She shrugged. "What can I say? There are a lot of elephant decorations in the world. Today I got sippy cups, and the handles are elephant trunks!"

He laughed. Then he kissed her again, and lingered on her lips. Her heart fluttered. It didn't matter how many times he kissed her—his lips were still miraculous.

"Thank you," he said.

*For the sippy cups?* "For what?"

He nodded toward his basketball team. "For

making me a better man. For making all my dreams come true. For curing me."

She grabbed his shirt and pulled him closer. Then she pressed her lips to his.

After several wonderful moments, he pulled away. "Heidi, there are children!"

She giggled. "I didn't cure you. The juices and herbs did."

He shook his head slightly, his eyes full of light and life. "I didn't even know I was lonely. But I was. And no herb was going to cure me of that."

# More Large Print Books
# by Penelope Spark

The Billionaire's Secret Shoes
The Billionaire's Blizzard
The Billionaire's Chauffeuress
The Billionaire's Christmas
The Rising Star's Fake Girlfriend
The Diva's Bodyguard
The Songwriter's Rival

## Penelope also writes as Robin Merrill
Shelter Trilogy
New Beginnings
Piercehaven Trilogy
Gertrude, Gumshoe Cozy Mystery Series
Wing and a Prayer Mysteries

Made in the USA
Columbia, SC
23 May 2025

58391823R00126